The Horus Perspective

An Egyptian Mystery

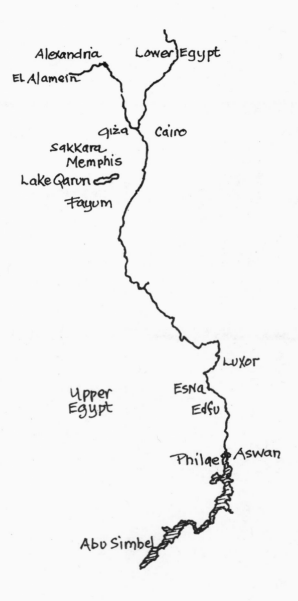

The Horus Perspective

An Egyptian Mystery

Shirley Surrette Duffy
Florence E. Freeman

This book is a work of fiction. Any resemblance to actual persons or events is coincidental.

Library of Congress Cataloging-in-Publication Data

Duffy, Shirley Surrette.
  The Horus perspective : an Egyptian mystery / Shirley Surrette Duffy,
Florence E. Freeman.
      p. cm.
  ISBN-13: 978-1-884186-39-4
  ISBN-10: 1-884186-39-4
  1. Americans—Egypt—Fiction. I. Freeman, Florence E., d. 2004. II. Title.
  PS3604.U379H67 2006
  813'.6—dc22

                                                    2006023040

Illustrations: Claire Young
www.claireyoungphotography.com

Hollis Publishing, Inc.
95 Runnells Bridge Road
Hollis, NH 03049
800.635.6302
HOLLIS
PUBLISHING books@hollispublishing.com

To
believers in the law,
"which is perfection of reason."

1

*Today is spent at your leisure. You
may wish to explore the busy streets
of Cairo on your own or simply relax
before your tour begins.*

The eyes were the bluest eyes Tina had ever seen. Blue eyes
in a brown face with white teeth and black curly hair. And
coming right at her taxi. A blue truck filled with brown-faced
men with black curly hair. All laughing. The blue truck had
veered at the last moment and slid past the taxi.

"My God!" said Tina.

"A near miss is as good as a mile," said Peter.

"Look out!" screamed Tina. A pedestrian half leaped over
the right fender and eluded contact with the car.

"I'd like to know the accident statistics," muttered Peter. "I
hope we get back alive."

The taxi switched lanes into oncoming traffic and back
again—a game of "dodgems," which went on and on. Peter
ground his teeth.

"I don't want to look," cried Tina, "but I can't keep my eyes away."

They were being catapulted down the main street of Cairo swaying in and out of the multitudes of humanity. Seemingly all fourteen million inhabitants of the city were pressed together on the sidewalks and the streets. Horns were in constant dialogue. The effect was dizzying.

"Look, look, look," half shouted Peter. "The Pyramids. Look." He pointed out the left car window.

Tina could see two pyramids to the left; they loomed beyond the buildings of the city; they were the past, the guardians of modern Egypt. To her surprise, the edges of the structures were clean cut, even after all the thousands of years since they had been erected. They were massive, enormous, tan and pink combined in color, cleanly and mathematically precise in the modern atmosphere.

The cab rushed by so quickly it was hard to focus on the structures. Tina said, "Maybe they're a wonder of the world, but they're of another world, another time entirely. They are not of us. You can feel it."

The sky of Cairo was not so full of smog as it had been earlier in the morning but there was that ever-present coppery hue with its translucent curtain of dust everywhere. An amber lighted stage setting, unreal and eerie. Even the smell of the desert was beginning to have a distinctive odor as if all the bodies of the mummies, all the food of the centuries, and all the myths of the Gods had blended with the dust of the earth and created an essence which, once experienced, was unforgettable. Occasionally, there was the kind of haze created by construction machines kicking up the dust. Front-end loaders were working in the valley between the road and the Pyramids. At least they were something concrete, part of a familiar world.

The street divided and the road they followed curved to the left, around the Pyramids.

"Welcome to Egypt," said Peter, as he leaned over and gave his wife a kiss.

Tina snuggled close to him, rubbing her cheek against his. She whispered into his ear. "Drop dead, darling."

Tina and Peter, two lawyers from Ohio, had taken time off for a holiday and this was their first day of leisure. Rising late they had hired a guide, who was supposed to speak English, to drive them to an oasis called Fayum, located sixty miles southwest of Cairo.

The driver, constantly grinning, took that moment to look back at his passengers and speeded up. Tina gasped. There was less traffic as they left the main road. Now there were no buildings and they were below the level of the Pyramids. Twenty feet of layered desert rose beside them as they drove. The road was straight, two lanes, desert on both sides. Real desert. Brown, without moisture, without vegetation, without green—light tan brown, deadly dry. God forbid that anyone get caught out there without proper supplies and water.

Although the driver still exceeded any speed limit conceivable to a reasonable person, Peter and Tina began to relax.

"You look chipper this afternoon," said Peter. "Three o'clock in the morning, lost luggage and airport confusion not-withstanding."

After arriving in Cairo, and having to wait at the airport for hours while lost luggage for their tour group was located, Tina and Peter had finally reached their hotel, disheveled and exhausted. At that point, they had difficulty knowing who was in the group and what the hotel really looked like. And here they were, after little or no sleep, seeking an oasis called Fayum.

Peter pressed Tina closer to him. Tina relaxed against his body. She loved her husband, his premature gray hair, his turned up nose so like the little boy she someday hoped to have.

"For a while there," she murmured, "I thought we would find an early grave. I never thought, somehow, to die in Egypt."

"And you see you haven't."

"Not yet. Fayum is still miles and miles away." Could there really be a flowering countryside and whirring waterwheels in the middle of a lifeless desert?

To the right of the taxi now appeared on the horizon a rather vast collection of low grayish-brown buildings. Peter leaned forward to have a better look while the cab continued in its express mode.

"I wonder if he speaks French," said Peter.

"We know he doesn't speak English," replied Tina.

Frowning, Peter speculated, "I'm curious about those buildings. They look like tombs. You know, like the cemeteries in New Orleans. This civilization seems to have been obsessed with death."

He remembered what he had read. That death to the ancient Egyptian was the continuation of life as he lived it on earth. Thus, much time was spent in preparation for the afterlife. Embalming alone required a minimum of seventy days. The dead were thought to be alive as long as they had human semblance.

"Parlez-vous Français?" Tina raised her voice to the driver.

He turned, grinning from ear to ear. "No speak English," he said.

"Watch out!" exclaimed Peter. "Jesus! He'll take his eyes off the road and we'll end in a ditch."

"You don't have any confidence in our chauffeur."

"You bet I don't!"

"City of the Dead," exclaimed the driver. He pointed to the right. "City of the Dead. Many peoples, one million, two million. Children. Women. Men. Place they live." He followed those words with several sentences in Arabic.

"Remember the movie *The Egyptian*?" asked Tina. "The hero worked with the priests in the City of the Dead. Learning about embalming and poisons and that kind of thing."

Peter frowned. "Do you think he means the women and children live there now? Maybe it's the old City of the Dead but living people have taken it over."

"That's gruesome," said Tina.

"Well, it's shelter," said Peter. "Better than sidewalks, probably."

The taxi whipped around a curve and the driver slammed on his brakes. The road was blocked in front of them and six or seven uniformed soldiers, fully armed, stood at both sides of the highway. Peter and Tina slid forward in their seats, then pushed themselves back.

"Roadblock," said Peter.

The cab hardly hesitated and went through and on its way. No words were even spoken. However, the driver seemed relieved. He pulled out a pack of cigarettes, turned, and offered some to them.

"No, thanks," said Tina, then continued aside to Peter. "There're too many soldiers with too many guns, to my mind."

"And another thing," said Peter. "There are too many cigarettes and too many people smoking them."

The driver scratched a match on the steering wheel, lit up, and inhaled with great pleasure. Peter and Tina waited for him to cough but he didn't. The driver waived his right hand indicating down the road. "Fayum!" he said and smiled.

"I should hope so," said Peter. "That's what we're here for."

But Fayum did not appear. The desert continued. Brown, tan on gray. Lonesome, without feature identification, without human or animal occupation. Except for one thing. Marching from horizon to horizon, sometimes close to the automobile as they drove, sometimes at a distance, came high tension electric wire installations. If one looked quickly or were restricted in one's view, this could be the United States Southwest or northern Mexico or some parts of the Australian Outback.

The group in the automobile was silent. The driver kept his eyes to the two lanes of the road; the passengers looked out the windows. Peter wondered whether the battle of El Alamein had taken place in the vicinity but could not figure out how to put his question to the driver. The inability to communicate irritated him. His life and that of his wife depended on communication. It was not without connection, he thought, that the practice of law became ever more lucrative and popular in the United States at the very time new and more inventive means of communication appeared on the market.

Tina clasped his hand in hers and rested her blonde head on his shoulder. The blue of his shirt emphasized the clear blue of her eyes. "Penny for your thoughts," she said.

"I was thinking about the law, our profession, and the growing speed of communication," he replied. Tina sat up with a start.

"Oh, for God's sake," she said. "Have you no soul, no poetry, no imagination—"

"Is that a tree?" interrupted Peter. "Look, over to the left. About ten thirty."

"It is—it is." Tina stretched her lithesome slender body forward and pointed. "And look! It's green—Over there. Those are real honest-to-God trees."

The driver turned his head around to face them. "Fayum," he announced proudly.

CHAPTER

2

*Fayum was the center of one of Egypt's most
ancient cultures. Its wooded countryside,
flowering trees, old waterwheels, and cultivated
fields offer a picturesque landscape in contrast
to the barren desert surrounding it.*

The trees grew into rows, row upon row, with cleared
ground between. Then agricultural fields came into sight,
flanking both sides of the road, with orchards in the background. There was the smell of lemons and limes and
oranges. They could see the evidence of productivity all
around them, not only in the fields but in trucks and stacked
wooden cases at the side of the road.

Tina and Peter were entranced. Green trees and flowering
landscape emerged before their eyes. It was fragile but lush at
the same time. "Who would have expected this!" exclaimed
Peter.

Tina did not answer. She stared and admired. Her eyes
darted from field to tree to orchard. The whole countryside
was moving in color—a rainbow of colors—bright fuschia,

golden yellow, electric blue, lime green. After the desert the scene before her eyes was difficult to believe. What is it about Egypt? she thought. It is a land of contrasts—of sudden changes—it is kaleidoscopic.

At first it seemed as if the tall grasses of the oasis were swaying in the breeze pouring out color like paint brushes, but, on closer look, one realized that bodies, real live human bodies, were slowly rising from the earth. They rose up gracefully, a few at a time, draped in beautiful colors, rhythmically moving across the fields toward home after a day of work—a medieval scene, unexpected in modern times.

It was the undulation and the leisurely attitude that mesmerized Tina. There was no rush, no quick movement. Only bodies moving, rustling the grasses in a suggestive way. There was plenty of time to contemplate what the evening might have in store. The bodies seemed to sway together in a universal language; the colorful soft cottons they wore flowed as they moved and outlined the contours of their figures. The whole earth was moving and in color.

"Peter," she murmured softly in his ear, "Is this our glimpse of paradise?" Peter, absorbed by the scenes outside the car, turned to her. "Peter," she repeated, "Perhaps we should have taken the advice of the tour guide. With a day of leisure we could have caught up on our jet lag." Peter tweaked the end of her nose and winked. "There'll be plenty of time!" he said. Tina smiled to herself and eliminated any further consideration of reading the numerous prurient advertisements which had come her way as a lawyer suggesting how to make sex life more interesting.

She gazed out the car window into the distance, dreaming her thoughts while watching bits of light begin to dot the horizon. Earth-color houses, low and small, could be seen everywhere. No obvious plan. They just happened. She wondered what went on inside these simple houses and realized she would never know.

The cab slithered around a curve, throwing her body against Peter. "Please get him to slow down," she said. "We can't see a thing!"

A donkey, carrying an overload of purple green vetch and an oversized rider dangling his long legs, caught her attention. The taxi was going so fast that there was hardly time to identify what the eye saw. A quick glimpse was all one could hope for. "No pictures, that's for sure," said Tina. They would have to stamp it on their own picture mechanism. If they could. The road was filling up with masses of people pouring out of the fields. Farm animals were sauntering slowly alongside their owners who switched them lightly to keep them under control. An occasional horse drawn cart piled high with boxes of citrus fruits zigzagged through the parading humanity. The taxi twisted and turned through narrow roads while the two of them twisted and turned trying to peer into houses—into darkened doorways. They drove through shady groves of tall and majestic palm trees, graceful cool umbrellas. And everywhere the green was accented with sudden color, contrasted against the approaching evening and the lowering sun. Happiness and contentment seemed to fill the air. Peter and Tina waved and grinned and turned their heads constantly to see this part of the fertile earth teeming with life.

The taxi slid unexpectedly to a stop. Peter's head hit the window. Dust rose around the wheels. They found themselves in the middle of a very busy intersection—the center of Fayum, they assumed. Opposite them was a railway station and an old fashioned railroad hotel. Because of the numbers of people, the sidewalks were almost impassable. Tina noticed the absence of women. Everyone was pushing for space, yelling and shoving. As soon as the occupants of the taxi were recognized as tourists, articles for sale were held out. Some salesmen banged against the taxi windows while others pushed their faces against the glass. Tina involuntarily recoiled against the seat.

"Boy, oh boy," said Peter. "I'm glad we're not out there."

"Oh, I don't know," Tina said. "It might be fun to be in the middle of everything."

"Let's take a holiday from being in the middle of everything. We're on our vacation, remember?"

"It's a carnival," said Tina, remembering that she didn't particularly enjoy carnivals. The faces against the window appeared to leer, their noses flat and the faces disfigured. They were all over the place popping up as if they were on pogo sticks. It was like magic. Tina began to feel fearful the way she always did at the "fun house" where the crazy mirrors distorted what one saw. She never giggled at the images the way her friends did. She felt stark terror. Was it she in those mirrors? What was the truth? And why was she always looking for the truth? Maybe that's why she became a lawyer. She was beginning to feel her heart race and moved close to Peter. She had changed her mind about wanting to be in the middle of all the activity.

"Lady, lady," yelled a grinning face, offering cheap bracelets. "Two for the price of one. Hurry before I change my mind." She found herself smiling in spite of herself. No doubt it was an expression he had heard from a tourist.

Suddenly the driver turned to them and said, "Come, come." They were at a loss as to what he meant until he opened the door of the back seat and beckoned them to get out. "Come, come," he said. He pushed away the bodies standing by the car door, and made ready to escort Tina and Peter somewhere. Tina actually felt some fear. But Peter got out on the street side of the cab and walked around the rear of the taxi to help the driver. Once again the driver repeated, "Come, come," and this time Tina left the automobile.

The early evening light was beginning to grow dim and the setting sun shone directly into their eyes. Tina felt a shiver. But they accommodated the driver by moving through the mob toward a gate and into an outdoor restaurant. They breathed a sigh of relief as their guide gestured toward a waterway with an ancient water wheel located in the center of the restaurant. Slowly the wheel turned and water cascaded over its scarred surface, sounding a continuous groan of exhaustion.

"We read about this," said Peter. "It's part of the irrigation system that early pharaoh had dug in here. You know, he must have been one smart politician. And it's still going today."

Tina smiled and walked closer to the water-wheel. It whirred and screeched its way through the water ditch as it had for so many thousands of years. Suddenly, their guide and a stranger emerged from the side room of the cafe. "Welcome to Fayum! May Allah guard your footsteps in our land." The speaker was the stranger, a slight, little man who spoke with the readily identifiable accent of Oxford or Cambridge. Tina and Peter turned to him in astonishment and he laughed. "I am the owner of this establishment and as you can hear I speak English rather well, thanks to the archeologists with whom I have spent many seasons. Now I am retired and make my living here. Please. Will you not sit down? Your driver tells me you have been asking many questions which he does not understand. Can I help while you enjoy some coffee—or perhaps tea for the lady?"

Tina and Peter exchanged glances. "I don't think we have time—" started Peter.

"No, we must get on," joined Tina. She did not want to prolong the trip. She was beginning to feel haggard and tired and a little bit itchy about getting back to the hotel. She moved closer to the water wheel and tentatively put her hand out to let the water drip through her fingers. The coolness was refreshing and she wiped her hand across her forehead.

"You are interested in the ancient water wheel. It is very, very old." He paused to collect his thoughts. "Most people think of Egypt and pyramids or golden pharaohs. We here are most famous for our wax painted portraits found on the mummies in the oasis. You realize our culture is quite unique compared with that Egyptian civilization closer to the Nile."

"We have been told about the portraits. Why are they special?"

The proprietor straightened his old school bow tie and launched into what was obviously one of his favorite subjects.

"The portraits found in Fayum appear to be death masks of real persons. They were made of wax and painted to resemble the actual pharaoh or what have you. They were not simply resemblances like the gold masks found elsewhere. As far as we know, no Fayum mask was made of gold, but should such be found it would of course be invaluable."

Tina's attention was drawn by the sound of voices from the other side of the water wheel. She turned away from the proprietor and stepped back in the direction of the voices. Through the falling water she saw a glint of steel. She dropped back another step to have a better view through the spokes of the wheel and what she saw stiffened her body in alarm. She had never expected to see such a sight outside of television. Seated at a small round table were two men. One of the men leaned forward, in the act of pointing a revolver at the other.

"Don't be a fool!" exclaimed the one toward whom the gun was pointed. He was an American from his accent. "I need you and you need me." He rose, his chair grating on the stones of the cafe floor. "It's my turn to be responsible for a change." He quickly picked up a partially wrapped, flat object which had been lying on the table between them. As he did so, the light from the setting sun caught the object. It flashed gold and illuminated for a quick second the two men, the table, and the gun.

The American, with great care, dropped the package into his briefcase and walked away. His darker companion stood, shocked, his hand outstretched, then, with a sigh, slipped the revolver into its shoulder holster. Tina had the presence of mind to note the American seemed the older of the two and that he was sandy haired, slender, and close to six feet tall.

"Come on!" called Peter insistently. Tina felt apprehension and tension literally in the atmosphere around her. Peter came to her and took her elbow.

"You should go now before it is any darker if you are to visit our lake," said the proprietor. "The ancient pharaohs hunted and fished there, just as we do today."

Tina and Peter followed the driver to the car. The crowd had dispersed and they sped off quickly toward their destination. As they drove away from the center of Fayum they noticed small fires being lighted in front of each house. Strange, with all the electric wire stretching across the town overhead. Tina decided not to figure this one out as she snuggled close to Peter, thankful for his protective presence.

Peter smiled as her head rolled on his shoulder and her eyes closed. He loved her. He held her tight in the crook of his arm while they journeyed quietly toward Lake Qarun. Without waking her he kissed her nose and rubbed his cheek against her hair.

Before they knew it they had arrived at a huge, dark body of water—an ocean of water. It was too dark to see anything other than the skeleton hulls and masts of dim sailboats, ghostlike on the inky water. Peter waked Tina gently to get a look before they turned right to the road which would take them back to Cairo. After a glance, she pushed closer to Peter and murmured, "So much for a day of leisure." She fell asleep again as they were emptied out into the blackness of the road north.

CHAPTER

3

The desert at night is cold and lonely.
Only ghosts are found there.

It seemed he could hear the sand singing against the wheels
and side of the automobile. The wind was rising and it was
reasonable to think he could hear the blown sand against the
car. Nothing was catching on the windshield but maybe it was
too dark.

No doubt about it—it was dark out there. No moon, no
stars. In the narrow light from his headlights he seemed to be
probing a dark cave, a black tunnel. His eyes flicked to the
rearview mirror. Nothing. No lights. No headlights following.
That was good.

In a sense he was running. From Fayum to Cairo. In
another sense he had succeeded. He felt the package on the
seat to his right. The rough paper was already familiar to his
touch. The paper contained the prize. His lips thinned in a

harsh smile. It was a prize all right. Just the gold, in weight, was a fortune in ounces.

And it was a work of art. God, was it a work of art!

Created by some unknown genius over five thousand years ago. Owned by rulers, captured by generals, traded for slaves and women's bodies. Now it was his. Not that he intended to keep it. He was not that wealthy. But someone else was and that someone else had promised enough for his retirement.

All he had to do was hold on. Or keep running fast enough. Of course, there were others after it. There always were. This was not the first time he had been involved in the secret transfer of objects, just below the surface of legal life, from one pair of hot, sticky hands to the next. It went on all the time. They called it the black market. And he had for years been part of those who traded in that market. This was his biggest deal yet. His hands gripped the steering wheel. It had to work!

He took a deep breath. Once again he checked the gasoline gauge. Listened to the sound of the engine. He looked to the sides of the car but could see only a few inches of white cement pavement unrolling in the reflected light from his headlights. He was alone in the desert it seemed. That was good.

He noticed suddenly, slightly to his left, at least a mile in front of him, a grouping of lights. He swore under his breath. Only about twelve more miles to Cairo and the hotel. Somehow that was safety. He slowed. He knew what it was. A roadblock. He felt rapidly in his coat pocket for his passport. Should he risk it? The diplomatic passport? If ever he was justified, this was it.

He slowed to a stop, opened the door to the car and stepped out. The uniforms closed in around him. Lights glinted on the heavy gun barrels, the oily machine gun belts. He held up his passport. High. And offered it to the most intelligent looking soldier. He prayed the man knew what it was. And he was lucky. The man came toward him, bowing and speaking respectfully. They could not understand each other. The soldier inspected the passport. He gave back the passport. He had actually had enough sense to check the picture against the man standing before him.

His breathing was easier. It took all his courage but he gestured, indicating he wanted to go to the bathroom. Several of the soldiers guided him toward an outhouse beside the road. There was some friendly laughter. He took care of himself as fast as he could and returned to his car. There it was. The newspaper wrapped package. All was well. He climbed back into his car and went on his way.

Once again the darkness and the automobile engine in the silence. Only, now, suddenly there were shots. A burst of machine gun fire. Then another burst. Without intention he slowed, looking in the rearview mirror. He could see what was going on. A car, without headlights, tried to go through the roadblock. He heard the gunfire, saw the headlights go on. The car spun off the side of the road beyond the troops and turned over. The road curved toward the emerging lights of Cairo and he could see no more. He realized his hands were shaking. He had not been alone on that road from Fayum.

4

*First night: Welcome cocktails and
a la carte dinner at the hotel.*

Peter and Tina, exhausted, dragged along the corridor to
their room in the Marriott. Peter slipped the plastic card
into the lock and opened the door. A white envelope lay on the
carpet just beyond the door. He picked it up and tossed it on
to the table by the easy chair. Tina slipped by him and collapsed onto the bed face down.

"Thank God we're back," she muttered.

Peter disappeared into the bathroom without saying a
word.

After a few moments Tina turned over, kicked off her shoes
and sat up to take off her sweater. The room was, typically,
similar to many American motels, Tina noted. It was, after all,
a Marriott hotel: light papered walls, thick green flowered
drapes, green flowered upholstery, not particularly exciting.

At the same time she applauded, mentally, the more interesting bed covers—green again but with a sort of Oriental-Islamic twist. Peter appeared in the bathroom door. "We've got fifteen minutes before dinner and I've got to shave. Do you want or can I go ahead?"

"Oh, I want. You don't really think I'm a camel." She patted his slightly rough cheek as she slipped by him. Peter began to strip off his polo shirt, T-shirt and loosen his slacks in order to change his clothes. Idly he picked up and opened the white envelope. His mind was on which tie he would wear for dinner but the contents of the envelope brought him abruptly to attention.

Facing him was a sheet of cheap paper upon which was pasted three sections cut from a newspaper:

NOT YOUR BUSINESS!

Without really thinking, he strode to the door, opened it and looked up and down the corridor. Nothing. The man who usually sat in the alcove to the left of their door was not there. And then he realized the envelope could have been left hours ago. They had been gone six hours on the trip to Fayum. As he turned and shut the door, Tina reappeared.

"What's that?" she asked casually. "Just as soon as I can I've got to take a shower."

Peter passed her the sheet with the pasted newsprint. "Someone has mixed up the rooms but what do you suppose is going on?" he said.

Tina read the sheet, turned to toss it on the desk and stopped in her stride. "I never told you! I didn't have the chance before I fell asleep—I know what that is." Peter put his slacks down on the bed. "At Fayum. While you were talking to the proprietor, I saw two men behind the water wheel. One was an American and one was probably Egyptian. The Egyptian was holding a revolver on the American but the American walked off with the package they had between them and the Egyptian let him. That's what this is about." She finished with certainty.

Peter's eyes narrowed as he thought for a moment. "I don't see how they could make a connection here. Did they see you?"

"There was no way they could miss."

"Just the same. They have to have us mixed up with someone else." Tina started back into the bathroom. "What the hell is going on!" exclaimed Peter. "I don't want you to get shot by mistake."

From the bathroom, Tina replied in a muffled voice. "It's going to take more than that to get rid of me." Peter finished stripping to his shorts and followed.

The noise of traffic and shouts in a foreign language became audible in the room; then there followed the sounds of the shower and water flowing in the wash basin. Americans are so clean. In Egypt, of course, no foreigner drinks the water. In fact, all tourists are advised not to open their mouths in the shower, let alone brush their teeth with tap water. Tina was careful not to swallow the water as she took her shower. Peter had finished shaving and was dressing by the time she dried herself and started to look for the clothing she wanted to wear for the evening. She wanted to wear her best on the first night. Her best was the flowered, pale yellow silk. "Beware now," said Peter. "You have to keep up the reputation of this place." He looked her up and down. "And you're not doing so badly."

"What do you mean?"

"We're living in a harem, aren't we? You have to dress accordingly."

"And what about you?"

"I'm the master. I am as I am," laughed Peter.

Tina slipped her dress over her head and turned to her hair and make up. "The Empress Eugenie must have had an extraordinary influence on foreign rulers. The khedive here rebuilt a harem for her visit—"

"And now the Marriott has rebuilt the reconstruction," interrupted Peter.

"Ready?" questioned Tina. And they went out into the corridor, found the elevator and descended to the lobby. The wood which framed the rooms through which they passed was dark and heavy, incorporating walls of veined marble. They went beyond the desk area to the head of marble stairs which led to the casino below. Tina gathered up her flowing skirt and put her arm under Peter's arm. As they descended the elegant and historic staircase, the treasure of the hotel, they looked like two storybook Americans—young, energetic, smiling.

They had no time for the casino as they hurried to the private dining room where their group was gathered. They were late and neither of them liked to be late. The tall, thin Egyptian standing at the double doored entrance to the dining room came forward with clipboard in hand. "Mr. and Mrs. Carson," he said, "It's good to see you. We're just about all here. Peggy Rufo, the Judge's granddaughter, and her cousin Dennis Frontiero are apparently delayed." He laughed. "They went shopping." He spoke excellent English. "My name is John and I am your tour director."

A stoutish, somewhat red faced man came forward. He moved easily on two crutches, or aluminum sticks, upon which he leaned. He seemed disturbed or out of sorts for some reason—until he smiled. "I'm Judge Poland," he said. "First night I ever spent in a harem."

A loud female voice interrupted from the background. "Boy, oh boy. Wouldn't it be fun to be in a harem. With all those men."

A white haired lady chimed into the conversation. "Mostly eunuchs." The female who had the loud voice tittered.

"Were you shopping?" questioned the Judge of Peter.

"We went off to Fayum," said Peter as he put out his hand to the Judge. "It was a real adventure. I have never seen such driving in my life. But fascinating—extraordinary—once we got there."

"How late do the stores stay open?" questioned the female voice. "I have seven grandchildren and they all have to have Christmas and birthday presents. I have to get busy."

"This isn't even the first day of the tour," commented a man from the background.

"I would suggest we hold any shopping until tomorrow," said John. "Unless you want to try the hotel. The shops here are open as long as the casino is open."

"I'm Joe Fairfax." A bearded man and the stout blonde woman came forward. "Bette has shopped the four corners of the earth and she still finds something to buy."

Tina replied to him. "I'm Tina Carson and this is my husband, Peter."

A tall, well built woman with crisply cut brown hair and horn-rimmed glasses came into the group carrying two champagne cocktails. She handed one to Judge Poland. "Here you are, honey. Enjoy."

"This is Polly," said the Judge.

Behind Peter, a waiter offered a tray of champagne cocktails. Peter picked up one glass and said to Tina, "Is this appropriate to the occasion?" Tina took her glass and toasted him silently.

The waiter passed to the white haired lady, who said to him, "I would appreciate another Coke." A gray haired woman to Tina's left joined in the same request.

Tina suddenly noticed a man standing by himself beyond the gray haired woman. He looked familiar. He was at least six feet with receding sandy hair. It took a second or two before she realized he was the American with the package on the other side of the water wheel in the Fayum cafe. Her heart gave a thump. The man turned toward her and before he could turn away she spoke to him.

"I didn't know you were on the tour," she said.

The man stiffened. "I don't think I've ever met you before." He took one step away. "Perhaps I remind you of someone. I'm a very common type apparently."

"At Fayum," said Tina. "The cafe—where the water wheel is. Or at least I think I saw you leaving the cafe there."

"The man interrupted her. "I have never been in Fayum in my life. You must be mistaken." He turned and walked away.

Peter, just behind Tina, muttered under his breath, "Take it easy!"

"If he wasn't the one at Fayum, I'll eat him," said Tina.

"I'll join you if we don't sit down pretty soon." Peter finished off his drink.

A Mr. and Mrs. Atkinson introduced themselves. They were from Texas, Austin to be exact. Their accents stood out from the Middle Atlantic states and the Midwest with which they were surrounded.

John turned to the Judge. "I think we should not wait any longer for your granddaughter and her cousin."

"I agree with you," said the Judge. "I don't know where they could have gone."

"Don't worry about them," said Polly. "They're all right. She's with Dennis and he'll look after her."

John turned to the tour group, which comprised eleven people, and raised his voice. "May I suggest we all sit down. Two of us have not arrived but I'm sure will be here shortly. We need to dine so I may have the pleasure of telling you about our plans for the tour."

Waiters appeared to help slide the heavy chairs over the thick carpet toward the table. The members of the tour took seats, first placing their drinks beside their plates. One waiter, with a gallant bow, picked up the napkin for the white haired lady and put it across her lap. She grinned and thanked him. There was silence for several moments while the menu absorbed all attention.

"The steak is probably the safest," commented Joe to his wife and anyone else who could hear.

"I'd like some Egyptian food," insisted Bette, turning to the tour director.

"Indeed, indeed," replied John. "The dessert will be an Egyptian specialty. It is an ancient delicacy, long a favorite of our people."

Tina noticed the man from Fayum had seated himself at the far end of the table from where she and Peter sat. She noted he was still wearing the same suit he had worn earlier and that the package he had carried away from the cafe was resting in his lap. His eyes would not meet her glance.

Two waiters appeared and began to take the orders for food. After soup and jellied shrimp, many of the tour group unhappily refused the uncooked salad. Places were then cleared for the entree and John rose to attract everyone's attention.

"On behalf of Wellington and Smith, Limited, it is my pleasure to welcome you to Cairo. Sorry to say, we've lost some luggage and Mr. Mott," he gestured to the man from Fayum, "has a bad cold." (Mr. Mott squirmed at the attention.) "But we are going to have the time of our lives—your lives."

As he continued, the waiters reappeared with the entree plates. "I warn you to get a good night's sleep because we start out first thing after breakfast. It will be served from 7:30 to 8:15 in this room. The bus will leave at 8:30 sharp from the Nile entrance to the lobby. After a quick tour of the university area of the city, we will go to the Museum of Antiquities, the foremost depository of Egyptian artifacts in the world."

The entree the waiters now served to the tour members was either steak or rolled chicken breast. Of course, Joe and Bette had the steaks, as did the Judge and Peter. John made no attempt to eat.

"An archeologist skilled in Egyptology will join us on the bus and after our visit to the museum and lunch at the Tara hotel, you will have the afternoon to yourselves."

"Tara, for heavens sake," said Tina in an aside to Peter. "I thought we sold Egypt munitions, not hotels."

The middle-aged gray haired woman on the other side of Tina peered over her glasses. "Maybe hotels would be more constructive." She winked.

John consulted his notes and continued. "Tomorrow night you may play at the casino if you wish, but we must arise early for the Pyramids and the Sphinx on Wednesday morning, ending the day with the Sound and Light show after dark."

Unexpectedly, in a moment of silence, as John drew a breath, everyone in the room heard the whisper from outside the door. "We're late. What are we going to do?" It was the voice of a girl, just a little slurred. "Don't worry. They won't fuck you," replied a man, half laughing.

The Judge rose, tipping over his water glass. His wife and Tina both reached out to catch the glass and prevent the water from spilling over everyone in the vicinity. Through the door-way of the room came a teen-aged young girl. Black hair in ringlets to her shoulders, shiny lipstick and too much eye shadow. The man with her was carrying his suit coat over his shoulder. His face was greasy, his head tilted to one side with a smirk on his lips.

"It's about time!" roared the Judge. "Do you realize—"

His wife cut him short.

"Peggy, come sit down on this side of the table. I'm sure they can rearrange the places." One of the waiters stepped forward to do just that. Dennis, the man with Peggy, went to the end of the table to sit next to Mr. Mott.

John continued as if nothing had happened. "I'm glad to see we're all here now. As I was saying, on Wednesday evening we will enjoy the Sound and Light show at the Pyramids, then go back to the hotel. We leave at 5:00 A.M. next morning for the airport and the Aswan Dam." There were groans.

As the meal continued, John having concluded his orientation remarks, the tour members exchanged comments on the weather, moves at bridge, and other pleasantries. They sounded like confident Americans at ease with themselves and their surroundings. The noise was not overwhelming, but it certainly would confuse anyone not familiar with American English.

The Judge's voice became transcendent over the noise. He was talking to John. "Human conduct can be quite frightening. I have known all kinds of cruelty, sadism." He stopped short to include Dennis in his glance. The rest of the table was silent. "The worst I ever saw—or really only suspected—was an example of cannibalism. Three kids lost up in the mountains. Only one survived. The Rangers never could find the other two bodies but they did find the bones. They were gnawed—"

Tina later could never remember what else was said as the girl, Peggy, slid slowly from her chair onto the floor. She had fainted. The Judge and Joe, together, pushed back chairs and knelt beside her. John clapped his hands sharply and the waiter in charge dashed for the door.

"I think she maybe had too much to drink," said John.

"She damn well had no business having anything to drink at all," said the Judge.

"I've sent for a doctor," said John.

Peggy sat up. "Dennis, Dennis," she cried. She reached out to get up. Dennis continued to eat.

The Judge and Joe helped her to her feet. The Judge held her. "I bet you didn't have any lunch," said Joe.

Bette put her arm around the girl. "You come up to our room and we'll get you some soup."

"Come on, now," said the Judge. "We'll get you into your own bed." The Judge, Polly and the girl left the room. John called for champagne all around.

Somehow the meal was finished. It was a perfectly good meal but no one present ever could remember what they had eaten. Nor did anyone say very much. Even Bette did not ask to go shopping.

As Peter was opening the door to their room, Tina finally put her thoughts into words. "I don't know whether we ought to ask for our money back or keep going."

"They won't give it back," replied Peter. He stooped to pick up another white envelope. "Now, what the—"

He opened the envelope and he and Tina looked at another sheet of cheap paper with newsprint pasted on it. It read

WE MEAN YOU

CHAPTER

5

A good tour guide prepares early.

The amber light of Cairo crashed through the morning into Hada Felous' bedroom, spreading its sharp rays across her bed. It woke her with a start. She did not resist its beckoning. This was a special morning. There was a smile on her face as she thought of what was to come.

She slithered one naked leg sensuously out from under the covers and drank in its shapeliness and its bareness. She reflected on its coffee color which pleased her sense of beauty. As she sat up, her black tousled hair, attractively unruly, bounced casually.

Today she would be facing a new group of American tourists whom she would be guiding through Egyptian history for two weeks. They would be seeing some of the most beautiful temples in the world. She liked guiding American tourists. She could wear her short skirts, keep her hair uncovered, and generally laugh and banter with these humorous and outgoing people who exuded a refreshing sense of freedom.

She could smell the coffee brewing in the kitchen of their four room apartment. She was filled with a sense of warmth and excitement—exciting for her but perhaps rather dreary for her husband and two young children while she was gone. Nevertheless they cared and supported her during these periods. She was lucky to be able to have this work. In school her first love had always been history. She could not contain her enthusiasm about the history of her country and became one of the foremost Egyptologists of her generation.

Being a woman was rather difficult. She yearned to become a college professor but circumstances prevented her from doing so. So she became a tour guide, which in the eyes of some could be considered a rather menial job. But in her eyes at all times, she was one of Egypt's great teachers. To know Hada was to know this.

As she reflected, she realized that she had some preparations to take care of before meeting the tour group. She hurried to dress carefully in order to make a good impression at her first meeting. Her dark brown skirt and tweedy brown jacket would be appropriate to the occasion. She glanced at herself in the mirror approvingly and then picked up her briefcase to count again the number of tickets purchased for the Museum of Antiquities in Cairo and to go over the list of participants once again.

As she was doing this, her husband Joseph knocked gently and opened the door. He handed her a steaming cup of coffee.

She smiled gratefully and passed a loving look over his face.

"Hada," he said. "I'll miss you during these long days and nights but I'm glad you have this opportunity."

She knew how lucky she was that he was her husband. "I hate to pressure you," continued Joseph. "But it's close to eight o'clock. Aren't you supposed to meet them on the bus at 8:15?"

She hardly heard him as she glanced over the list of the tour members. "Joseph," she said. "This is a strange mixture of people." Her voice was incredulous. "There is a judge, his wife and granddaughter from California. A single State Department man. Three lawyers. A retired college professor of literature from Massachusetts and—and two historians from Texas. And a couple from New York. What am I supposed to do with such a group? How can I keep them all interested?"

Joseph took the half consumed cup of coffee from her hand forcefully. She glanced at her watch in horror and dashed through the door, dashed back again as if she had forgotten something, gave Joseph a great big hug and kiss and said, "I love you. See you later—Bye."

Joseph knew she was already in her American tourist guide role.

6

This morning we visit
the Egyptian Museum of Antiquities
where you will see the fabulous collection of
King Tut Ankh Amun.

The room clerk was immaculately dressed, efficient but remote—not helpful. "Sorry," he said, "the only occupants we list for your room are you and your wife. Room 917. Is that correct?"

Peter rubbed his hand across his forehead in a gesture of exasperation. "Are you sure the room was not assigned to someone else originally? Maybe not someone from the tour at all."

The supervisor entered the conversation. "We do not understand your interest. This is privileged information. If something was left in the room—"

Peter almost lost his cool but Tina, standing next to him at the desk, interrupted. "There go the Judge and Peggy. I guess we're out of time now and have to get on the bus."

"Privileged information, my eyebrows! Why does he have to be so stuffy?" Peter fumed as they hurriedly went for the bus. "It's the only possible explanation for those notes. They were meant for someone else to whom our room was previously assigned."

"Relax, honey, relax. We're off for our first tour day. It's going to be exciting."

"I'll have to say one thing," noted Peter as he located members of the tour, "I'm thankful Peggy is up and about and with her grandfather. He's got to be a more suitable influence for her than the cousin."

"How old do you suppose she is anyway? Sixteen? Seventeen?"

They had reached the bus and the conversation had to stop. They were the last to arrive and the bus pulled away before they even had the chance to sit down.

John stood to introduce their guide. She stood beside him. Her name was Hada and she was a small going-toward-the-chubby Egyptian, a graduate of the University of Cairo with a special degree in Egyptology.

The streets of Cairo were already overfilled with automobiles and buses. The horns honked constantly and brakes squealed repeatedly. The morning smog was thick as long as the bus stayed close to the Nile but as soon as it moved into the academic area of the university the sun showed clearly. No one would be telling the truth to say Cairo was beautiful, but the old sections looked as one would expect one of the oldest cities in the world to look and the newer sections looked both French and English. Only the most recently built areas were constructed in quickly poured concrete.

Hada spoke excellent English and shortly it was obvious that she enjoyed laughing. She commenced with some history.

"During most of its existence, Egypt has been divided between Upper and Lower. Lower Egypt is symbolized by the papyrus and Upper Egypt by the lotus. Our social history commenced either 5,000 or 4,500 years ago. Once we thought we could clearly prove the First Dynasty began in 3100 B.C. The dating has now become precarious and we must allow for the possibility of error."

The bus came to a stop in the paved courtyard in front of the Museum of Antiquities. The eager beavers among the tour group struggled to their feet before the door was even open. Bette led the scramble with the cry, "They have a wonderful gift shop here. Stuffed full of real old things. Just think. If they're old enough, they'll be duty free."

Hada stopped the bus driver from opening the door. "Just a minute. We'll visit the museum first, then spend a short bit of time at the gift shop." Without waiting for comment she led the group past a time-eroded statue and into the museum. Tickets were presented and the Americans gathered together. Bette looked as if she could not understand why she was in the museum and not in the gift shop.

Peter looked up at the grand staircase in front of them and into the morning sun. He noted countless dust particles accented by the sunlight. Hada stopped in front of a group of pillars and with a small lighted pointer traced out the lotus and the papyrus at the top of the columns. "These obviously are stylized but, combined or separate, they permit us in many instances to date what we are looking at within certain broad periods. Just as the history is divided into dynasties, the dynasties are lumped together into the Old Kingdom, the Middle Kingdom and the New Kingdom. What we shall be seeing here, since we cannot see it all in about two hours, is largely in the New Kingdom and occurs in the Eighteenth and Nineteenth Dynasties or 1500 to 1200 B.C."

Peter stifled a yawn and wandered across the room to a display of weapons, spears, arrowheads and knives. His eyes were caught by the word "FAYUM" on the next display case. He signalled to Tina to join him and the two examined the contents of the case. What stood out, among other objects, was a life sized death mask. The lips were painted in faded red dye and the hand drawn eyebrows were black above the closed eyes. Tina whispered to Peter. "This is what the cafe proprietor was talking about."

Hada's voice rose above the din of the museum. "Tut Ankh Amun, the boy pharaoh, bodes large in Egyptian history only because grave robbers failed to find his tomb. Even the remains of Ramses the Second, our most egotistical pharaoh, were pillaged. And Queen Hatshepsut, the only female ruler, was virtually obliterated by her successor."

Peter moved on to the next display while Tina tried to keep herself within hearing of Hada and still hold Peter in the corner of her eye. It was not easy. Too many people were attempting to occupy too little space. There was pushing; there was noise and the sound of feet scraping on stone floors; school children ran through the crowd yelling in stage whispers; there was just plain conversation.

Tina began to be aware that Hada was looking more and more upset. She could see the blood rise along Hada's neck and into her cheeks. While she continued to lecture and walk from object to object, she looked back, over her right shoulder, again and again. Tina attempted to follow her glance and moved away to her left, away from both the tour group and Peter. Suddenly, she saw what Hada must have been seeing. It took her breath away, too.

In a corner, partially hidden from view between pillars, Dennis had Peggy pinned against a squat limestone sculpture. Her feet barely touched the floor and her body was stretched on the worn stone. His forearm held her head back and successfully muffled any screams. With his other hand, he pushed

Peggy's clothing further up around her breasts and lunged forward into her. Tina could see his erection from where she stood. She thought she heard a groan from Peggy, but then was baffled as she watched Peggy's body writhe in rhythm with Dennis' movements. If anyone looked, they turned their heads away in embarrassment. Largely no one paid any attention. Tina started to turn away herself. She was aghast. She was doing nothing either. Her only thought was to reach Peter. She looked around, saw him, and ran in his direction. It seemed as if all of Cairo got in her way.

Bette, of the yellow sweat suit, loomed between Tina and Peter. "How would you like one of those for your dining room," commented Bette. "Just the thing for stuffed mushrooms, huh?"

Peter and Tina both looked around wildly. "What? What do you mean? Where?" Tina was almost beside herself but she could not dislodge Bette who now had Peter by the sleeve to pull him into the tour group to see what would hold mushrooms. Peter laughed.

"Peter!" cried Tina. "Come here, Peter, come here." Still laughing, Peter grabbed Tina and pulled her with him into the group. Tina cuddled up to him as he put his arm around her, and bent his ear to hear what she wanted to say.

"Peter! What do we do? Peggy is being raped—I know she is."

"What? What?" responded Peter. "I can't hear you."

"I said—"

Someone set off what sounded like a forty megaton bomb in the basement. Everyone jumped, then laughed as nothing happened.

"Never mind," finished Tina. She twirled away from Peter and the group and found herself looking into a display case at a golden colored mask which gleamed in the sunlight. It attracted her attention but she had no time to think. Coming toward her were Peggy and Dennis. Peggy's head leaned against Dennis' shoulder. She was smiling. His right hand was under her skirt and she appeared to make no objection. Tina felt almost sick and humiliated for Peggy. Where was she coming from, anyway?

Peter stepped up to Tina, from her right. "Now, what were you saying?"

"Too late now," said Tina.

"Tell me anyhow," said Peter.

"Later. When we have time. A terrible thing just happened."

Hada's voice, raised—she was close to shouting—cut through the noise. "We're going up to the second floor now. The second floor is dedicated to the objects, largely gold, which were found in the tomb of Tut Ankh Amun. Don't touch anything, try to handle it or lean on any display cases. For obvious reasons everything is wired for security. Neither you nor I want to interrupt our day at the police station. There are rest rooms to the right of the stairs as we go up. If you get lost, find the famous solid gold mask of the king. I shall keep an eye out for you there. I don't think you can miss it. The mask is the one you have seen pictured so often."

The group started up, straggling from step to step. Mott and another man, from a different group, disappeared into the men's room. Tina saw Peggy head for the women's room and decided to follow her.

The wash room was a pleasant surprise. Apparently someone had visited in America and brought back the decor: well lighted, tiled walls in oatmeal, tiled floor in Wedgwood blue, and, when she got that far, American Standard fixtures. The room was not crowded. Peggy went into one cubicle and Tina waited. She washed her hands. And waited. She dried her hands. And waited. The room emptied. Only Peggy and Tina remained. Then Tina heard little hurt animal sounds. Peggy was whimpering, very quietly, but she began to interweave her little puppy cries with sobs. The sobs became more and more out of control, deeper, almost gasping. Tina began to be alarmed. Hesitantly, she approached the cubicle door behind which Peggy was gasping for breath. She knocked.

"Peggy," she said. "I'm Tina. You met me last night, at dinner." The sobbing stopped. "Peggy? Are you all right? If you want, I'll go back to the hotel with you. You can tell me what's wrong."

She paused. There was no sound. After several seconds the toilet flushed. Tina tried again.

"We're all exhausted. Not enough sleep and now this mob scene. Would you like to go back to the hotel with me?"

The door opened and Peggy flung herself out. She pushed by Tina and out the door. Tina had enough time to see that her hair was in disarray and her eyes and nose red and wet. Tina paused in shock before she pulled herself up to follow. Outside, on the stairs to the second floor, there was no sign of Peggy. Tina realized that in some way she had said or done exactly the wrong thing.

It was hotter on the second floor of the museum. There was no air and the dust seemed thicker. Tina thought for the first time that one impression she would carry with her about Egypt was the dust and the airlessness, the dryness even close to the banks of the Nile. She looked around her to seek either Peggy or some member of the group. She walked along down the main lane between exhibits, following the surge of the crowd. Ahead of her loomed the golden bust of Tut Ankh Amun. It dominated the room as it was meant to do. Behind it and on the walls at the side were displayed photographs of the excavation with portraits of the important archeologists. It was then Tina heard Hada's voice. She was apparently answering a question.

"Of course, there were curses and promises of death for those who might violate the sacred tomb. We are very certain that by the time of Tut Ankh Amun grave robberies took place regularly. One might comment that the robbers paid as much attention to the curses as do twentieth century archeologists."

Tina saw Peter and smiled. She moved through the crowd to his side. He took her hand and held it. "Let's move along here to the right," said Hada, "to the tomb houses of the grave. You see those black objects. They are hollow and fit down, together over the tomb. There is one door. You see there, on the first one."

The tour group moved down the left wall beside the death houses, following Hada toward a door at the end. Tina, look-ing down at the floor as she paused behind the middle-aged gray haired woman, was momentarily puzzled by a streak of dampness which crossed into the tomb house enclosure and around to the other side. Then she realized what it was. She was looking at the marks of wet shoes in the dust on the floor. Peggy's! she thought. She had sought refuge in one of the houses, that one, beside them.

Tina waited until the group was almost out of sight, looked around for a guard, saw none, and slipped under the cord around the house. She walked between the houses to the other side and peered in at the door of the nearest house. It was open a crack. She was not surprised to see Peggy curled on the floor at the back wall. She slipped in through the door and walked over to Peggy.

"You know you can't stay here," she said. "When they close you will be found and will have to go to the police station." Peggy looked up wildly and moved as if to run again. Tina decided she would catch her this time. But Peggy simply stood there. The water of her tears was running down her face. Tina had never seen anything like it.

Peggy took a deep breath and pushed her hair back from her face. "Don't tell the Judge! He and Polly want me to have a good time. What can I do. Oh, what can I do!"

Something stopped Tina from saying she had seen the whole scene with Dennis. Later she was glad she had kept that information to herself. Now she put her arms around Peggy's shoulders.

"Whether you like it or not I think we should go back to the hotel."

"I don't like it here," cried Peggy. "I want to go home!"

"That's thousands of miles away," said Tina. As she spoke she felt like a fool. She had to do something to help. "Let's go back to the hotel. We can have something to drink in my room. And then we can talk about what's bothering you." She smoothed Peggy's hair, who shook her head and her shoulders sagged.

"I guess I've got to. What else can I do? Whatever you want to do."

Tina realized suddenly that something had broken Peggy, long ago. She had no fight; she went along with what was proposed. Her reaction to Dennis and what he had done to her became more understandable.

Tina half slipped her arm around Peggy's waist as if to support her. "Come on then. We'll get a taxi and go back."

In the taxi, across the lobby, and up in the elevator, Peggy maintained a stony silence. Tina opened the door of the room—only to be greeted with a rough and tumble bed, just the way she and Peter had left it, his pajamas on the chair by the desk and her suitcase open on the luggage holder. No one had appeared as yet to make up the room. Tina's heart sank. Out loud she said, "Why don't you go out on the balcony while I straighten things up a bit. It's a beautiful view."

Peggy said, "Yeah," and went over to stand by the open sliding door onto the balcony. Tina whisked all loose clothing into the closet, flipped back the bed clothes and discovered she was perspiring. She wiped off her face with a towel from the bath and turned to Peggy. "Now we can sit down." She indicated a chair. "What about a spritzer? It's early, but so what." Peggy did not reply. Tina called downstairs for room service and put in her order. Peggy finally came back into the room and slumped into the chair. Tina seated herself on the corner of the bed. Peggy looked down at the floor and Tina looked at Peggy.

"This is a difficult conversation to begin, isn't it?" She questioned agreeably. Peggy grunted. Perhaps in agreement and perhaps not.

"Is your mother still alive?" In Tina's experience mothers either were a solution or part of the pain. Peggy's head came up and she spit out her words. "You bet. A nuclear holocaust wouldn't get her. She loves to say 'the good die young.'"

"And your father? Why didn't he come on the trip? At your age my father and I were inseparable."

"I'll bet."

"But the Judge is taking the place of your father. On this trip anyway."

"If you say so."

Tina studied Peggy with narrowed eyes. This was really being very clever. Most adults would have thrown up their hands but Tina was not one of them. Peggy was not going to get away with it. Tina had faced recalcitrant witnesses before.

"When did you lose your virginity?" she asked coldly.

Peggy looked up, startled. Her mouth opened, then closed. She turned in her chair and looked around the room before answering. "Last year. At the junior prom. Every one was doing it. The boys like it and I don't get left out."

Tina did not miss "I don't get left out." She thought she saw her approach. "You're a senior now."

"Yeah."

"In high school."

"Yeah. Where else?"

"Oh, I thought one of your experience and maturity might well be in college." Tina could see Peggy almost expand in her pride. "Are you using the Pill?"

"Yeah. I steal them from my mother. She never knows the difference."

"She is popular, too."

"You bet. They're getting a divorce. Pop says he won't stand it and Moms says he'll pay through the nose. She's trying."

Tina was almost sickened. "Are you planning on college? Are you a good student?"

"I used to be," replied Peggy a bit sadly. "Dennis is going to help me. He's going back to school, too. He's real big on education."

Mark one for Dennis, thought Tina. There was a knock on the door. The spritzer. Tina swore under her breath, "Damn." Just when she was getting somewhere. But she went to the door, admitted the waiter, signed for the order, saw him pour a glass for Peggy and one for her and saw him out with the appropriate tip. She went back and sat down. Her sip of the Campari tasted cool and refreshing. Not bad. "You must have your hands full with the boys from the prom as well as Dennis."

"Well, Dennis really. In the museum, even, he made love to me. He doesn't leave me out. The Judge likes me, too, but Polly keeps a close hold on him. Moms says he has a reputation."

In Peter's overused expression, thought Tina, "Jesus Christ, what next."

There was more knocking at the door. Before Tina or Peggy could move, the door was opened wide to reveal two men, one with a pail full of detergent and rags, the other with a vacuum and a mop. The room cleaners. Peggy rose with a scream on her lips. Tina put her arm around her and led her onto the balcony.

"They're just here to fix the room," she said. She was astounded to feel that Peggy was shaking. She turned to look at the Nile in the noon sun and directed Peggy's attention toward a boat just below them. "It wouldn't take any imagination to believe you could see Cleopatra coming down the river to meet Marc Anthony."

Peggy had stopped shaking and moved away. She leaned on the railing, looking down at the boat. She was crying again, silently, effortlessly. Tina realized suddenly where she had seen crying like that before. Her secretary, years ago, just before she had had a nervous breakdown. But where in Cairo, Egypt, on a warm afternoon in January could you find a good psychiatrist for adolescents? Tina felt a stab of fear. And at the same moment she heard the Judge's voice.

"There you are. Polly and I didn't know what could have happened to you."

CHAPTER

7

After breakfast we drive to the ruins of Memphis . . .
Nearby is Sakkara . . . whose fourteen pyramids include
the ancient Step Pyramid . . . built about 2680 B.C.

"Oh, I just love Egypt." It was Peggy, replying to a question from the gray haired woman. "It's so different, you know. It's awesome."

"I have to find time to arrange for some imports. That's for sure. I'm in the business," said Dennis, standing behind Peggy in line for the bus.

The Judge shifted his weight from one crutch to the other. He was frowning at the ground and finally lifted his head and glared at Dennis. The gray haired lady showed interest. "What kinds of things do you import, Dennis?" she asked.

Dennis cleared his throat. "Oh, you know, ladies' garments—with mystique." The Judge snorted at the answer.

Peggy giggled and took Dennis' hand to swing it back and forth.

"Are they sexy, Dennis?" It was Bette, hoping for the best. Voices were high-pitched and fast-paced. The tour group was beginning to let its hair down and a tone of familiarity could be heard in the erupting conversations.

"Thank God, I remembered my old dark glasses," commented the white haired lady to no one in particular. "The new ones have simply disappeared."

"For Christ's sake, Bette, move your butt onto the bus or you'll be responsible for us missing the Pyramids." It was Joe.

Bette, dressed in polyester pink with the latest style jodhpur pants, was squinching along, her fat thighs impeded in their movement by the tightness of the pants and the straps which held them even tighter around the feet. She was waving her fingernails and blowing them to dry the fresh plumwine paint which had just been applied to match the outfit. She squealed as only she could, "Eeeee, I can't wait for those Pyramid souvenirs. Bobby would just love a stuffed camel and they've got to have little paperweight pyramids for school—Joe, where is my journal? Have you seen my journal? I must write down every detail. And I hope you've got the camera. Did you bring the camera, Joe?"

Joe scuttled ahead, pretending not to hear, while the white haired, heavy set lady slid past everyone as fast as she could in order to get a seat in the back of the bus, as far away from the group as possible. She was most gracious about it, smiling all the way, and speaking to everyone as she very cleverly maneuvered her way around.

At the other end of the bus, Hada, the tour guide, was wearing a look of resigned tolerance on her face. She had been through it all before. Some would be bone weary and let you know it. Some would have hangovers from too much Egyptian wine; some would be heaving in the nearest toilet from gyppie tummy and hold up the bus. And some would just plain not show up.

By this time, Bette had managed to hoist herself up on the bus, where she was spread out on the inside front seat. Joe, lugging all the extra gear for both of them, collapsed on the seat beside her. His shirt was already damp from his efforts.

Another squeal was heard out of Bette's rosebud mouth, thick with plumwine lipstick to match her nails. "Oh, Joe, here comes that impressive Mr. Mott. See if he'll sit across from us."

"Fat chance, Bette. Have you seen him talk to anybody yet?"

"But he's so mysterious. It always intrigues me—you know. It's a kind of challenge to figure out what's going on underneath." She dropped her voice. "Don't you think it's fun to try? Especially when he's sooo mysteeerious."

"If there's any figuring out to do, you'll do it, Bette."

"Do I detect just a wee bit of criticism in your tone?"

Before Joe could answer, Wilbur Mott was standing beside their seat. Bette leaned over Joe, all smiles. "Hello, hello, Wilbur. Have you been shopping already?" The response was predictable. None.

Wilbur Mott switched a package from one hand to the other and turned his head away from Bette while proceeding to the back of the bus. Bette called after him. "You have too been shopping." Mr. Mott ignored her. At first it appeared he would sit down beside the white haired lady, with whom he usually exchanged nodding glances. He sensed her respect for privacy matched his own and continued on until he found his own niche and settled in with a look of distance about him. He placed his package carefully on the empty seat beside him.

Hada busily applied herself to counting noses. She asked if everyone was present. No one answered. She wondered aloud if she had the right list. Everyone seemed to be too occupied to pay any attention. She sighed.

Bette verbally accosted Peter and Tina as they made their appearance at the door of the bus. "I was wondering if you were going to make it." Peter and Tina stepped quickly onto the bus and found seats across from one another with the aisle in between. Peter bent over and mumbled in Tina's ear about wanting to come back again someday on his own—minus the group—in order to be able to look and think at his leisure. Mr. and Mrs. Atkinson, the authors from Texas, followed by the Judge and his wife, Polly, completed the group.

"It's quite a mixture of people," said Peter to Tina. "But I wonder about the Judge. He runs hot and cold. Nice guy. Still at times he looks really worried and I've noticed him churning in anger."

"I guess if you had to get around in this hot climate on crutches, you might be a little upset, too."

Tina and Peter noticed Hada counting again. There seemed to be a problem. She was getting one more person than she was supposed to have. "Did anyone change his mind about coming? We have one too many." A hand was raised and an unfamiliar voice explained that he belonged to the other tour group but wanted to catch an earlier ride to the Pyramids. As Hada walked down the aisle of the bus to speak to the stranger, the bus lurched forward. They were on their way.

The bus maneuvered its way through narrow streets. The interesting shops were alive with business. At times the bus roof had to scrape between overhanging branches of trees which were growing in an unruly fashion. There was little conversation on the bus now. Everyone was intently looking out the windows. No one wanted to miss anything.

"We are on our way to see one of the seven wonders of the world." Everyone turned to Hada, who was, in her firm and serious way, beginning her lecture on the Pyramids. You could tell she was proud of her heritage and enthusiastic about the information she was giving the group. "The three pyramids of Giza are the most important of all—along with the unique structure of the Step Pyramid."

The silence was broken. "Hada, how do you spell Giza?" yelled Bette, who was writing in her journal. Then there was the snap snap of cameras—trying too hard to focus on everything in sight. A disdainful look crossed the face of Wilbur Mott.

"There they are. The wonders of the world. The Pyramids." The white haired lady spoke in a hushed tone of voice. The massive monuments seemed to rise right out of the rooftops of Cairo. The bus turned down a street and the pyramids could be seen no more. Groans of disappointment could be heard from the group.

The bus windows were open part way and pungent odors were more obvious than usual. These were the delicious spicy smells of food that were becoming so familiar in Egypt—and so elusive—mixed with those of the fresh green of growing things near the Nile. And yet, there was an ever constant film of fine dust carried through the air in evidence that the desert was always close by. Handkerchieves and Kleenex were in use at all times to combat the grit covering everybody and everything.

Wilbur Mott's voice was heard in a rare moment of speech. "Does anyone have a Wipe 'n Dri? This damn dust is unbeatable. Reminds me of my days in India. I can't keep up with the Kleenex—and this nasty cold on top of it."

Most people pretended they didn't hear, but the white haired lady fished around in her Coach handbag until she found something suitable for the one in need.

Hada, the guide, continued. "The Pyramid evolved from the mastaba during the Third Dynasty, under the influence of the sun cult. During the First Dynasty, the pharaoh was buried in an earthly replica of his palace. But later the concept evolved that the dead Pharaoh could now ascend to heaven, so he must be placed in a tomb that would allow him to do this. Some theorize that this Pyramid was laid in steps so he could ascend the stairs to heaven. Later the steps were filled and the Pyramid resembled the cone of the sun's rays as they poured down upon the earth. Since these Pyramids were to be 'houses of everlasting' they naturally become larger and larger in order that they would be able to contain everything needed for eternity."

Bette, who was trying to keep up her notes in her journal, twisted uncomfortably. Joe stifled a yawn, weary from being bounced around trying to balance all the gear that Bette usually brought along or bought on the way.

"At Giza, one of the Pyramids built by Cheops covers an area of thirty-one acres." At this point, Bette was clearly becoming frustrated. "Cheops" was too much for her. She would wait for the interesting stuff to write down or respond to the spicy stuff. She put her pen back in her purse while she glanced out the window for a change. The buildings of Cairo were now beginning to recede in the distance behind them. The bus heeled and took a sharp left. There, unexpectedly this time, within easy viewing range, upon a rocky plateau sat the three Pyramids of Giza. The yells and whoops of delight were not to be squelched. Hada did not have a chance, although it was clear she was not to be defeated by a bunch of yelping American tourists. She continued gallantly. "There is a story that Napoleon sat beneath the shadow of this Pyramid, the one nearest us, the one known as Cheops, and stated that the structure before him contained enough stones to build a wall around France ten feet high and one foot thick." The tour members exchanged glances of disbelief.

"I didn't know Napoleon was in Egypt, Joe," exclaimed Bette. Mr. Atkinson, the historian, swallowed the wrong way and began to cough.

"I don't believe it." "Look on the horizon." "Camels, real live camels." It was hard to tell who was making the comments. "I want someone to take my picture sitting on a camel." "Better watch out. They'll take you for a ride." The bus overflowed with chatter.

Slowly the bus chugged up the hill, on a long dirt road, its dust covered hood aimed for the sharp edged monolithic constructions standing against the horizon. The tourists were overwhelmed by the size of what they saw, but it was not what one would call structural beauty. For those who had seen the grace of the Grecian temples, the Pyramids came close to being a shock. The thought was inescapable that it took thousands of workers and no one knows how many deaths to build just one. Yet, the real wonder was that man could by primitive means accomplish such a task.

It took time for the enormity of what they were looking at to sink in, to be assimilated. The mood changed suddenly when the bus came to a grinding halt at the foot of Cheops. The vehicle was quickly surrounded by vendors in colorful dress, all yelling simultaneously in bastard English, in an effort to sell some scruffy souvenir to the innocents from America.

"Joe, they've got Pyramid souvenirs. Some money! Quick! Come on. Come on." As she leaped from the bus, there was no doubt in the minds of the vendors who would be their first victim. The others were quickly trying to make their way off the bus to take it all in, but Wilbur Mott seemed not to be of the same mind. In his polite, almost British manner, he let everyone else go first while he scrutinized the scene before him. Was he bored? What was he looking for? After all the jabbering tourists had found their way off the bus, Mott followed. Wind seemed to be blowing in all directions. "A good omen," said Hada, which seemed strange since the main preoccupation of the tourists, aside from waving off grimy salesmen, was trying to see through the grit and the sun.

"Joe, my sunblock and sun hat in the backpack—quick—the sun is blinding—and you know with my delicate skin I'm a sitting duck." Bette was on Joe again. "Did I forget my sunglasses and, Christ, where is the Deet? I sure as Hell don't want to go home with a case of malaria." She turned to the gray haired woman. "I refuse to swallow one more malaria pill. They wreck my appetite." Joe was about to respond but didn't. Discretion is the better part of valor, he thought. Bette did not hear the silence.

The group started to separate. Some headed for the camels who were decked out in gay-colored fringe and tinkling bells. Mrs. Atkinson, who merely wanted a picture of herself sitting on a camel, found it didn't work that way. As she sat on the saddle, the camel rose up tall and started to gallop away with her. She screamed, frantically waving her arms and legs wildly before being rescued by a very adept grinning camel owner who thought it a great joke. The physical jolt was as great as the cost of the ride. The limping victim decided to take a rest and go back to the bus to readjust herself.

Meanwhile, the white haired lady was taking advantage of the situation to quiz Hada and get as much background information as possible. She stuck closely to her, raising questions about the architecture and history of the Pyramids. She had never revealed her profession, but it was clear that she was not only interested in the past, but knew a great deal about it. She made the guide feel appreciated.

Suddenly, in the silence of the desert, martial music came to the ears of the group. Looking into the distance they could see marchers and dancers stepping rhythmically around the base of the great Sphinx. The majesty of the scene before them was unexpected and fascinating. A few yards from the pyramids sat the Sphinx—an awe inspiring sight. The Sphinx who represented centuries and had been buried by the sand for ages before being dug up by Chephren. The Sphinx with the body of a lion and the head of a king. The Sphinx which had been used as a shooting target in the nineteenth century but survived. The Sphinx, two hundred and forty feet long and sixty-six feet tall. The whole experience had a mystical aura about it which would be difficult to verbalize or to forget.

Many of the group stood solemnly trying to absorb all the sights and sounds around them. They knew they would be returning that night for the great sound and light show to be held here. But there was no more time now to contemplate the scene. They were later already than the schedule allowed for. They had to move on to the Step Pyramid, a short distance away, and continue to the Mena Hotel for a special luncheon.

A very hungry bunch, a bit wearier than usual, boarded the bus for the short ride to the Step Pyramid. Mott, who had stayed close to the bus, led the way up the steps. At the pyramid not a few of the tourists seemed to suffer from depression—or was it exhaustion? There was another reminder of death in the very structure which symbolized the fruitless efforts of the Egptian nobility to prolong its existence. The wind had turned temporarily cold and a thin cloud layer had intercepted the sun.

The gloom was lifted slightly by the continuation of Hada's lecture. This time it was the kind of lecture that would command rapt attention. The group huddled together to listen. One could see in the distance the houses of Cairo while between the horizon and the group two camel riders rode together, their animals and bodies silhouetted against the sky.

Hada started describing in gory detail the life and death of a mummy. To start the process the mummy was left standing in the deep chamber of the tomb. After its viscera were removed and placed in jars and sealed for posterity; after its heart was taken out, weighed and replaced; and after its brains were forced out through its nose with a hook it was walked around its tomb as if living. Hopefully it weighed no more than a feather so the body could proceed to heaven.

The Americans were horrified but hypnotized by the graphic description. Bette commented to Wilbur Mott, "What rubbish." There was no reply. Mrs. Atkinson inquired for the ladies room and was directed to the lean-to at the far side of the Sphinx.

Still trying to engage Wilbur Mott in conversation, Bette turned to discuss the mummy procedure with him. "Wilbur, doesn't it just turn your stomach? I'll never be able to eat lunch after hearing that."

Wilbur turned away from Bette. A single crack was heard from the distance. Wilbur was thrown against Bette then catapulted to the ground. He sat up immediately, holding his arm while blood started to pour out of his sleeve. The package he had been holding lay on the ground beside him. The crows screamed in the silence.

"Jesus, what happened? Wilbur has been shot!" There was chaos from the tourists. The Judge pointed in the direction of one of the camels and its rider going toward the horizon. The rider disappeared while everyone rushed to the aid of Wilbur.

"Don't move, don't move. We'll get the ambulance—You're bleeding all over the place." Wilbur picked himself up, spurned any aid and dashed to the men's room at the side of the Sphinx.

"Let him go," said the white haired lady. "I don't think he's badly hurt. He wants to take care of himself. He needs to be left alone for a bit."

Hada was obviously upset. She stated to everyone, twice, that she had never had such a thing happen before. It would be dreadful if it got into the international news. Several of the tour members got the impression that Hada might lose her job. Still Mott did not appear.

Hada gave him several more minutes before checking on him. She stood on one foot and then the other. Finally, when he did not appear, with great determined strides she went to the lavatory to retrieve him. She swung open the door while calling his name, only to be met with the sound of the wind whistling through the silence. He was gone.

8

*We will enjoy a relaxing lunch at the Rubayat
restaurant in the historic Mena Hotel.*

The environment had become alien and the group's appre-
hensions were obvious.

It was a shaken lot which boarded the bus. They were to
have lunch at the Mena Hotel, a world renowned hotel, one of
the most popular in Cairo. The luncheon was to be special—
a time when everyone would have a chance to relax and taste
the best of Egyptian food. With a member of the party not
only hurt by a stray bullet, but lost to boot, no one quite knew
what to do. Everyone tried to be cooperative. The silence was
deafening and Hada was wearing an expression seldom seen
on her face, one of panic. She hesitated, counted heads again,
and said that she and the driver would scan the area once
more before leaving—and to stay put.

No one argued. They stayed put. But in the silence, while the wind whipped the sand around the bus, there were many unanswered questions. First glances, then whispered short comments, then body movements displayed the uneasiness present among the tour members. They watched as Hada and the driver went in opposite directions trudging wearily through the hot sand and glaring sun making the effort to find their missing member.

Hada called out, "Mr. Mott, Mr. Mott," as if some Egyptian God would arrive to help. The two bodies became smaller and smaller as they faded in the distance, looking hopelessly minute against the massive pyramids.

Bette could stand it no longer. "I guess we'll be late for lunch. My God, what a time to get shot."

Peter became sarcastic. "I think you'll live, Bette. A human being's life may be in danger."

"Could they have carried him by camel to a hospital—or put him in the truck we saw?" questioned Tina.

"That sounds reasonable," answered Joe. "If we don't get moving, I'll have to find a tree somewhere."

Everyone screamed wildly. The closest resemblance to a tree trunk would be a camel leg. The tension of the group was relieved somewhat.

"Thank God," said the Judge. "Hada's turning back and beckoning to the driver to do the same." Up to this point he had not indicated any concern whatsoever. His attitude seemed to be "Let's get this over with. It's hot. I'm hungry." Perhaps his legs were hurting. He had been moody all morning. It was not clear why.

Hada and the driver returned. Sweat was running down Hada's beet red face. She was attempting to restrain herself and remain calm. Noting her condition, the group became concerned for her. As soon as she was on the bus she announced,

"We shall continue on to the Hotel for lunch and I shall call in Inspector Hakim to assess the situation."

"Who is Inspector Hakim?" asked the white haired lady of Peter.

The bus started to roll slowly down the gritty, sandy, dusty road toward Cairo. It, too, seemed to reflect the heaviness of its responsibility. One less passenger unaccounted for was not an everyday occurrence. But wait! There were two less. Where was the other tourist who had hooked a ride with this group? Did he get another ride back? No one asked but the white haired lady could be overheard mentioning it to Tina and Peter. They did not make an issue of it, and the Judge who was sitting close by shrugged his shoulders. The bus continued to roll, leaving behind a whole history and culture that reeked of as much mystery as Mr. Mott and his disappearance.

In Egypt, visitors become very quickly aware of the juxtaposition of life and death, dispensed as quickly and easily as a Coke from a Coke machine. Perhaps Inspector Hakim, whoever he was, would indeed shed light on what was happening.

The passengers twisted and turned to get a going-away glimpse of the Pyramids, a "wonder of the world" mixed with camels, salesmen, and twentieth century slang. An incredible mixture and for thousands of years capable of an overwhelming impact on the human mind. The "wonder" word often used to describe the Pyramids was an apt one.

As the bus nosed into the driveway of the hotel, there was a dazzling change—a scene of hilarity and color everywhere— flags flying, fashionable clothes, dripping jewels on necks, on arms, on ankles. Everyone seemed to be part of a scene straight out of a Hollywood film. And trees! Someone yelled, "Hey Joe, there's your tree! Take your choice."

There were huge copper pots filled with gorgeous, tropical flowers, the kind of pots and plants that would make an

American household jealous. The kind of decoration which one would like to see in one's own living room. The excitement was catching and the group started to babble as usual, as each one popped off the bus and seemed to regain a second wind. They almost forgot about the Mott episode.

"I need a good stiff drink," said the Judge. "Anyone join me?" Peter and Tina and the white haired lady quickly joined him. He was always good for a few laughs with his wit, and some wonderful stories about his work in California. Those who could moved in his direction and felt fortunate to be part of the orbit.

"Christ!" yelled Joe. "My eyes haven't adjusted to the dark yet. Do I see who I think I see standing by the bar holding a drink?" All heads turned to see Mott with his State-Department posture, a drink, and a package on the bar beside him. The disdainful and pale look he was wearing did not invite warm greetings or questions of concern. Extreme resentment poured forth from the group. Joe, with condemnation in his voice, exploded to Bette, "What an asshole."

Hada did try to show concern. She moved toward Mott to ask what had happened. His response appeared to be as casual as his stance. But he took a step back and awkwardly thrust his arms behind him, fumbling with the package as he did so. A forced smile and a sudden twitch of the face belied the seeming nonchalance. "After washing up I caught a ride to the hotel so I wouldn't miss lunch. Hope it wasn't too much of an inconvenience." He took a sip of his drink. "I did tell the white haired woman to ask you all to wait."

The white haired lady looked astonished. The look on her face plainly told the story. It was not true. But she did not bother to respond.

"Gallantry does not come easily to him," commented the Judge quietly.

There was no apology, no explanation, nothing that one could get a grip on. But the gray haired woman, who was standing beside him, was close enough to detect a taut, grim look about his eyes. There was something about him that she did not understand. She moved closer to the white haired lady. "When I stood by him, he seemed to be actually afraid."

The white haired lady replied, "He was shot, you know. I'd be scared, too."

Hada, whose patience had been tried to the utmost, and who did not understand Mott's lack of courtesy, wheeled about and said, "Inspector Hakim will be here to investigate the shooting incident. We are all concerned and puzzled about what happened."

Meanwhile, Peter and Tina and the Judge tried to restore the group's equilibrium by moving toward the huge luncheon buffet and urging others to follow. The sight was unbelievable. Enormous mounds of fruit, vegetables, meat, fish, desserts.

The choices were overwhelming. Thirst provoking pineapples, juicy honeydew, mingled with ripe red watermelon. Sliced limes, oranges and bananas were displayed on banana leaves. Vegetables surrounded stuffed chickens, turkey, mountains of roast beef, delicately colored fish, salmon mousse— and on adjacent tables appeared fresh figs, dates, nuts, and mouthwatering desserts too numerous to mention. The colors, aromas and anticipated tastes were dizzying.

Bette breathed hard and attacked the food with moans of delight. She described each bit she put on her plate, insisting everyone try her choices. Plates were heaped and for the most part the conversation turned to food.

But there were those who sidled over to the white haired lady to let her know they were furious about Mott's callous dismissal of their concern and especially his attempt to put false responsibility on her shoulders.

Tina said, "Wouldn't you know the State Department would slink out of it."

Just at that point a pudgy, slightly balding, wide-eyed, genial looking man appeared on the scene. His eyes bulged with delight as he grabbed a plate and alternately filled it and his mouth while announcing that he was the Police Inspector. He stuffed his mouth as full as possible. No one paid too much attention to him as he played the role of unconcerned observer. They were all eating, munching, laughing, and relaxing after a taxing episode. Hada walked up to the huge wheel of food and joined the Inspector. They moved in tandem, pretending it was not a serious moment. Hada leaned closer to the Inspector and bent her head toward him slightly as she mumbled into his ear. He listened intensely, suddenly stepped away from the food, put his plate down, and, with an authoritative tone, pulled himself up to his full height and announced clearly, "Is there a Wilbur Mott present?" The chatter ceased. A hush passed over the room, and all eyes turned in the direction of Mott.

He was standing close to Bette. He turned and appeared to bump her accidentally, causing her purchased packages to cascade about her on the floor. He apologized for causing her to drop her bundles. As he helped her pick them up she thought, "God, is he clumsy." But she straightened her hair and skirt, conscious of his attention.

Joe questioned, "Got everything, Bette?"

"I think so, Joe," said Bette. But she was puzzled over a strange looking package that she found in her hand and did not recognize. She turned to Joe to ask him what it was but decided she'd check it out later, maybe in the bus while they were going to the next museum. The thought of another museum dragged her face down. More shopping would be fun—but another museum? The Inspector moved closer to

Mott, lifted his arm, saw the bloody sleeve, and put his hand on his shoulder to comfort him. "I need to take you to the hospital. My car is right outside. You need to have that looked at." Mott straightened and tried to back away. The group watched quietly as Wilbur Mott, trying to protest, disappeared with the Inspector.

"What next?" said Peter. "This is turning out to be an unbelievable vacation."

"Sweet and sour," said the Judge. One suspected this was his judicial cover-up—intentionally ambiguous.

9

Speak justice, do justice . . .

Despite the exotic food and luxurious surroundings, Mott's wound and subsequent conduct could not be ignored. The mood of the tour turned sour.

It was a droopy group which wandered around waiting for the next move. Hada attempted to snap them into focus. "We shall board the bus for the Solar Barque Museum—a sight not to be missed. The funeral boat of the pharaohs." The announcement did not lift the spirits of those present.

"More death and darkness—and mystery," whispered the gray haired woman to Peter, who was standing alongside her.

The tour members took the same seats on the bus as they usually did. Some had left packages on their seats instead of carrying them into the restaurant. Bette, who liked to drag hers around, now darted for an empty backseat to drop her bundles. As she dumped her load, her attention was again caught by the strange looking package. She hesitated, then decided to peek under one section of loose paper to see what it was. Oh, my God. She almost exclaimed aloud. The package was not hers. It was gold, solid, thin gold, and seemed to have face-like features. She turned to Joe, but instinctively said nothing. Something told her to be quiet for once. She worked the paper shut, and quickly took her seat. She would discuss it with Joe later.

The tour group napped as they bounced along the highway. Those who were awake saw more dust and another hill to climb to the entrance of the museum which housed a huge funerary boat recently excavated near the Giza Pyramids. The process of rebuilding the Barque was still going on. They got off the bus, and went through the usual procedure of getting their tickets at the entry gate.

Walkways were built on two levels around the boat in order to provide exterior and interior views of it. One by one they climbed the stairs to the ramps.

Hada started. Her voice was not as strong as usual. "The Dead, in order to reach the heavens, had to be taken to the Underworld in order to pass a series of tests to prove their right to enter the promised afterlife. The Underworld, which ran parallel to the Nile, and under the cities, was a dark and fearful place haunted by monsters waiting to devour those who did not qualify. When the suppliant was deemed worthy of immortality, Horus took him by the hand and led him to Osiris who would allow him to continue his life in the sky."

Trudge, trudge, trudge. Six pairs of Reeboks scraped along the ramp feigning interest in Hada's words. In fact, if one looked above the Reeboks, one could hardly see any distinguishing characteristics of dress. Sweats, loose-hanging tops—the American health-exercise look of the late twentieth century. The expressions on some of the faces were similar, too: bored, though trying to get their money's worth. Others looked more enthusiastic; it would be important to repeat this story accurately back home.

Slithering up on the Reeboks was a shiny pair of dark brown Cordovan loafers. Above the loafers, no sweats. A crisp looking, white linen suit with a pink ruffled shirt peeking out, green agate cufflinks showing below the sleeves. It was Dennis, still completely out of place. He was obviously vying for attention and he was getting it. With a cocky, smirky look of conquest playing about his face, he sailed past the whole group, picked out Peggy, and stood with his arm around her. He could not be missed. The group looked at him with disgust. They were too tired to cope with his intrusion.

Hada looked frustrated. "Since we're late we'll have to shorten our stay here. We go next to the Sound and Light Show of the Sphinx."

"Good," smiled Dennis. "I'm right with you."

"Jesus," said Tina to Peter. "That guy has colossal gall."

"He's obviously trying to push a few buttons, and he's doing it. It's a wonder he has nerve enough to show his face—"

A loud stomping of crutches was heard trying to catch up with the group. Polly was heard to warn, "Easy, Judge, these slanting ramps are quite tricky." Always with the Judge in mind first, she quickly caught up with him and was ready to grab in case he slipped.

"Why in Hell do we get caught in places like this! I'm going to wait outside next time."

Hada tried to stir up more enthusiasm by continuing to impress the group with the history of the most significant boat of its kind ever found. "As you know, the Cheops Museum is fairly new, built in order to preserve this great archeological find, which is nearly forty-five centuries old and in excellent condition."

Dennis pretended interest. "Look at the size of this damn thing. It's longer than the Queen Elizabeth." He smiled, satisfied with himself. Peggy looked all giggly and proud that Dennis should know such a thing. They snuggled and nudged each other like kittens playfully making new discoveries about their bodies, or teenagers love-punching and slapping. Only Dennis was no teenager. He had to be in his late thirties, anyway. Out to impress the chicks with his green agate, tasteless cuff links which jarred the color combination of his outfit.

"You know so much," simpered Peggy.

Bang! A crutch slammed into a cement pole. "Are you all right, Judge?" inquired Hada.

"Hell, yes," grunted the Judge. "Let's get out of here and on to the next place."

Everyone moved a little faster to get back on the bus, while Peggy and Dennis played an adolescent tag game. The Judge looked as though he would explode but Polly restrained him with her calming manner.

It was late afternoon and after the long and emotion-filled day, exhaustion set in with the group. Some were discussing abandoning ship and returning to their hotel for the night; some pulled themselves together to go to the Sound and Light Show at the Pyramids. The group thinned out and only a few stalwarts remained to see what was billed as the first and one of the greatest shows of its kind in the world.

As remnants of the group arrived at the site, they were late. They discovered it was cold and the atmosphere was eerie. After climbing stairs in the dark, tripping into one another, they hurried to the seats and tables set aside for viewing. The seating was managed but soon after they sat down everyone was grumbling about the cold weather. It dug into their bones and they bundled up with whatever they had available to keep warm.

Dennis yelled to the waitress for two hot beers. Giggle, giggle. He leaned close to Peggy and played with the wisps of ringlets around her face. Peggy's eyes half shut and she sighed in her pleasure at his touch. She whispered in his ear. "I love you."

Bette blurted to Joe. "You'd better not get any beer. You'll have to find another tree and there ain't none. Only a sphinx and three pyramids."

"Funny, funny, Bette. This better be good. I'm frozen and dead tired."

"You heard how good it is, Joe. We couldn't miss this. Shh, everybody," whispered Bette dramatically. "The lights are going out. Ouuuuu, it's spooky."

A swelling voice vibrated across the desert and began to sound its overblown note of doom. It was coming from the vicinity of the Great Sphinx—the lion with a human head which was said to have held a statue of the pharaoh Chephren between its paws. But time had obliterated many of its features and its paws were being completely restored.

"I read that this particular Sphinx had been buried by sand for years," Peter repeated to Tina. "He promised a long reign to the Pharaoh who dug him up."

Tina looked down at her coffee. "God knows what else is hidden under this sand."

The voice rolled out its message:

Speak justice, do justice,
For it is mighty;
It is great, it endures,
Its worth is tried,
It leads one to reveredness.

"Bring on the dancing girls," mumbled Dennis under his breath. "I want my damned money's worth."

The Sphinx continued:

> When Goodness is good it is truly good,
> For justice is for eternity:
> It enters the graveyard with its doer.
> When he is buried and earth enfolds him,
> His name does not pass from the earth.
> He is remembered because of goodness
> That is the rule of God's command.

"Oh bull," muttered Dennis. "We've had enough of this." He pulled Peggy by the arm. "Come on, Peggy. Let's hit the night spots of Cairo."

The sphinx was illuminated by a theatrical flash of lightning: a huge crack of thunder followed. The Judge slammed the table with his crutch. No one breathed.

The show continued. Warriors poured onto the stage in front of the Great Sphinx with shouts and clashing of swords. Trombones heralded their arrival and lights flashed on the Pyramids, the face of the Sphinx, the desert, the audience. Attention was riveted to center stage. A blinding red light illuminated the whole of Giza. The tour group was jarred out of reality into some realm of horror. Bette screamed, "Joe, are you there?"

For some, the frightening illusion of the present was becoming more threatening than the past. As the light provided the opportunity to look around, the Judge tried to find Peggy and Dennis. He glanced in all directions. It was difficult to move easily with crutches and the extra clothing hampering him. He pulled himself up to get a better look. Peggy and Dennis were missing. He slumped back down in his chair with a calculated narrowing of his eyes. Polly put her arm around him with a sigh.

10

Transfer by plane to visit the Temples of
Ramses II and his favorite wife Queen Nefertari.

Like an ancient dirty rug, the desert rolled out beneath the airplane. At times the plane played with its shadow; at times the shadow slipped aside. There was always the desert. Its colors changed but were unchangeable: mustard, tan, dirty brown—and dry. And sand, sand, sand. The port wing lifted and the Nile could be seen, a thin green line of vegetation surrounding a blue-tan streak. It was a twisted green, its oxbows twisting through the dry land and off into the distance.

For over two hours they had been flying beside the Nile or crossing over it, back and forth. Their destination was Abu Simbel, the temple complex of Ramses the Second. For about the fifth time Tina propped her eyes open. It was all she could do to keep awake. Wake up call had been three in the morning. She hated to get up in the dark. She never could go to bed early and sleep, not that they had had the chance to go to bed early. After the wounding of Mr. Mott, his disappearance and reappearance, the arrival of Inspector Hakim, the fearsome impact of the red-rust Sphinx at the sound and light show, and the disgusting relationship of Dennis and Peggy. Yesterday had simply been too full. She had not slept at all.

Suddenly her eyes caught a glimpse of a tiny building below. Its color was lighter than the surrounding desert. It appeared to be built around a kind of courtyard. It had to be a temple. Maybe the building was Abu Simbel. Tina turned to Peter to point out the dot below. But Peter was asleep. Tina let him sleep. She looked back to the ground and the temple had disappeared. She closed her eyes, just for a moment—and slept.

The plane flew on. Its elevation was 20,000 feet, then fifteen, then ten. Abruptly there was a steep bank to the left. It crossed the Nile and descended rapidly. Tina awoke with a start. Peter grunted. Bette's voice was immediately audible. "I'm worried about him! He definitely was not at the airport and he is not on this airplane. Someone needs to be concerned and no one is."

Hada's voice cut in. She was seated just behind Tina and Peter. "If your concern is about Mr. Mott, he is with Inspector Hakim. The Inspector had to check Mr. Mott's file. He has promised to return him to us either at Abu Simbel or certainly by the time our Nile boat sails."

Peter was awake again. Under his breath he murmured to Tina, "Look at the fortifications." He pointed his finger. "Over there and to the left." Scooped out under the low-lying, moundlike hills were what had to be airplane hangars. On the starboard side of the plane, where Tina and Peter were seated, there had to be at least eight fortifications.

Peter commented to Tina, again in a low voice, "Consider the mess, the horror, if the Aswan Dam went. No wonder the Egyptians have protection."

The plane came to a halt on the blacktop and robed figures in turbans rushed out. They shoved into position the platform steps to the plane and the group disembarked.

In the waiting room twelve sleepy Americans lined up to be inspected by the Egyptian officials and checked off at least three different lists. The heat was distinctly present. It was humid, yet very dry and dusty. Tina did not stop to think of the contradiction. Then the bus was ready and everyone was glad to sit and rest a little longer.

After a short tangent down a relatively new but narrow road the tour bus (a Mercedes this time) came to stop in a parking place behind a group of low hills. Hada gathered the tour group around her at the side of the vehicle.

She began her commentary with a smile. "It is pleasant to talk about people helping people. You may remember that in the course of the planning for the Aswan Dam, it was realized that once the structure was in place the water of the Nile would shortly fill in many meters deep behind the completed work. Many temples and ruins would be drowned." Hada cleared her throat. "A call went out from archeologists all over the world, not just Egyptians, to raise money to save Abu Simbel and Philae. We will visit there tomorrow." She paused. "The money was forthcoming and the two treasures were saved. The temples were cut up in sections and moved several kilometers to new sites where they were reinstalled. If the Pyramids are an ancient wonder of the mind and labor of men, to the credit of the modern world the saving of Abu Simbel and Philae represents a glimpse of what we can achieve in concern for one another today." She turned to lead the way toward the hills. "So now let us go to see what our generation has done with the work of Ramses and his architects and slaves."

Tina's glance was caught by the figure of the Judge. His right crutch almost went under him in the sand. His wife leaped to his side but he recovered himself. Peggy stood with her back to the rest of her family. Dennis was within arm's length of her but not touching her.

Tina watched Peggy as she moved away with the group. Her thoughts reverted to her conversation with Peggy in the hotel room. She remembered with great disquiet how Peggy's tears coursed down her cheeks without any muscular effort. It was not normal and Tina knew it was not normal. Her instinct told her Peggy's emotional stability was very fragile. She could not be certain that Peggy was responsible for what she did. In her opinion the young woman needed expert help and the sooner the better. At the same time she was not sure she should discuss her thoughts with the Judge.

Tina locked hands with Peter and the two trudged along with the others across what appeared to be the usual desert sand of Egypt: dirty sand, small stones, and dry soil. Peter stopped to take a picture and the two fell behind the others. Looming to the left was a fair sized hill. The others of the tour went around the hill and disappeared. Tina heard Peter swear and she knew what the trouble was. The camera had jammed. Peter waved her on and she hurried after the others. She was about to round the projection of the hill when she heard angry but controlled voices in front of her.

"I won't have it! I brought her with us to have some normal pleasure." It was the Judge. "Maybe you haven't had her in bed yet but that doesn't mean you're not trying! Dennis, she is a child! She is not quite sixteen. And don't tell me I'm naive. You know damn well I'm not!"

"We're in Egypt. Remember? How old do you think those dancing girls are? The very ones you slobbered over in the casino last night."

"Don't try that on me," threatened the Judge. "I can destroy you utterly and don't you forget it."

"Yeah. Yeah. I hear you."

The Judge's voice changed. It was the voice of a man who was accustomed to being obeyed. There was arrogance, cold steel, authority. Tina had heard that tone before. He said, "You will go to the ticket office when we get to the airport, after we see Abu Simbel, and get yourself a ticket home. I never want to see your perverted face again."

Peter came up on Tina from the rear and barged right around the corner of the hill to a position in front of her. Tina had no time to catch him. She had to follow him. What they both saw did not reveal what had gone on. Dennis was simply walking ahead of the Judge, off toward the shoreline of a lake.

The water was blue. The wind blew up faint whitecaps and fine sand. Tina and Peter turned their heads to the left to avoid the dust—and there it was. Ramses, four Ramses. As high as a four story building. In front of them the Judge turned to go toward the gigantic statues; Dennis continued toward the shoreline.

"Whew!" exclaimed Tina, "You missed it!"

"What do you mean?"

Hada called to them from about a hundred yards away. She waved her arm and they hurried to catch up. She always stopped her lecture until those who were lagging behind came up with the group. Peter slowed to stay with the Judge.

As they came within earshot Hada had started again.

"On your left is the Great Temple of Ramses II and on your right is the temple of Hathor, dedicated by Ramses to his favorite wife, Nefertari. Look at the third Ramses from the left at the Great Temple. Look down his right leg and you can see Nefertari. Notice that she is three times her actual size but still only comes to his knee.

Tina swiveled on her heel. The view took her breath away. The lake on one side and the two hills supporting the temples and statuary on the other. Somehow, modern archeologists had managed to preserve the vastness and dead glory which must have been at the original site.

Tina noticed Peggy had joined Dennis at the edge of the lake. Her hand clutched his arm as he spoke vehemently to her.

He tried to break away and she tried to prevent him. He said something and Tina was startled at Peggy's reaction. She put out both her hands to him and Tina could see the tears glistening on her cheeks.

Hada pointed to the Temple of Hathor. "Notice Ramses and Nefertari are the same size at her temple. This is the only example of such equality for a pharaoh's wife."

Peter leaned close to Tina. "What was going on?"

"The Judge ordered him to go home. I mean ordered!"

"It's about time. I gather he doesn't know what has been going on."

"Not completely," replied Tina.

"If he did, I wouldn't blame him for killing Dennis."

Hada started the group toward the entrance to the Great Temple. "You cannot use your cameras in the temple because of the damage which might be caused from flashes. And there is not enough light today to take pictures naturally. So put your cameras away and enjoy the marvelous craftsmanship of the sculptors. What you are looking at is the work of many craftsmen, completed at least 3200 years ago at the height of the Nineteenth Dynasty."

The middle aged, gray haired woman took out her field glasses to have a closer look at the carvings and statuary above the temple entrance. She exclaimed, "Look up there! Look at all the graffiti. But look how nicely it was done!"

The Judge interjected his comment. "It's so neatly done, I'll bet the authors did not appreciate what they were marring."

Peter glanced at the Judge. "Still a crime, though, Judge."

The Judge pushed his dark glasses straight on his nose. "Probably it was not a crime at the time it was done."

The tour group passed into the temple.

The interior was chilly and dank. The floor was of sand and rising from the floor to the lofty ceiling were Ramses—in the plural. As one passed from the entrance to the sanctuary at the very rear of the temple, it became apparent that the walls of the temple and the ceiling had once been covered by magnificent frescoes. In the greenish light one could catch a glimpse of the actual colors in the frescoes. There were hints of crimson and blue, gold and imperial purple. Of the statuary or the frescoes Tina much preferred the frescoes. Among the figures, prominently displayed, of course, was Ramses, but with him were a number of gods and goddesses, bowing and offering him respect.

Peter rested his hand on Tina's left shoulder. "Can you imagine what it must have been like to be THE PHARAOH? Even the Gods honor him. We live in the age of the common man. But once the only people who lived were the rulers and their hangers-on. The rest were so much—so much—sand."

"Do you suppose there's anything so equalizing as a ladies room around here?" asked Tina.

"Are you all right?" immediately queried Peter.

"I'm perfectly O.K. No problems. I'm just a human and not a god, I guess."

Peter patted the top of her head. "I thank my God for that!" They both moved in the direction of Hada who was standing by the altar-like stone in the sanctuary. The Judge and his wife were standing with her.

"He can get his tickets changed, then, right here."

"There should be no problem," replied Hada. "Dennis and I can go together to the ticket officer. But isn't that too bad! I thought he was being so kind and thoughtful with Peggy.

However, unlike ancient Egypt, business is business and especially in the United States."

"Yes, especially in the United States," inserted Polly.

Tina interrupted. "Hada, I hate to return to today, but is there a ladies room around here somewhere?"

"Oh, of course! That's the best thing that came out of the archaeological renovation." She raised her voice. "After we go to the Temple of Hathor we shall go behind the scenes to view the interior of these two man-made hills. They really look like airplane hangars. But in the meantime if anyone wants to use the sanitary facilities, go out around this temple to the left and go in by the first door. It's marked W.C. in the British manner. Join us at the Temple of Hathor. I won't let the bus go without you!"

Tina handed her pocketbook to Peter and strode off, as instructed. She turned around the temple to the left, saw the door marked W.C., opened the door, and went in. Somewhat to her surprise she was in a long corridor. She walked to the end, noting doors to the right and to the left, but none was identified. At a loss to know what to do, she began to try the doorknobs on all the doors. The first two on the right were locked; the first on the left was locked; the second on the left opened. She stepped into a rather large and not well lighted store room—or little used laboratory. No ladies room, for sure. She turned to leave when her eye was caught by movement at the other end of the room. A figure was climbing up on some boxes, then the figure put something around its neck—Tina needed to look no longer. She ran as fast as she could the length of the room and seized the figure around the waist.

"Oh, no you don't!" she screamed.

Tina had Peggy around the hips, trying to hold her in position to prevent her from placing her weight on the noose around her neck. Peggy twisted and kicked but Tina held on. She realized she could not save Peggy from herself very long.

She looked around, in so far as she could, to try to find something with which to sound an alarm. The only possibility appeared to be to knock over the boxes and storage containers within the reach of her hips. She tried and knocked over what turned out to be a tin container. She was lucky; it made a loud tin-clang. She shoved sideways at another box and was lucky again. The box landed on the floor with a loud thump, then rolled and knocked into another container. Tina let go of Peggy for a second and swept all the glass containers on the counter by her side onto the floor. The smash sounds went on for several seconds. She began to shout. "Help! Help!"

And again she was lucky. She heard a body slam into the room and the body spoke English. It yelled, "What the hell is going on?"

"Help me. Help me. She's trying to commit suicide. I can't hold on much longer!"

Stronger arms than Tina's caught Peggy around the waist and Tina was able to let go.

"Get the rope away from her neck," panted the man. Tina climbed up on the counter and removed the rope from Peggy's neck. The man put her down on the floor and Peggy collapsed into a limp mass at his feet.

Tina immediately knelt down beside Peggy. She put her arms around her and said, "It's all right. It's all right. We all love you. Believe me, we all love you. You are not alone. This happens. We love you. You are not alone."

At first there was no response. Not only was there no response but Tina could not tell if Peggy was breathing. She looked up at the man who had helped her. He looked down at her, then indicated with a shake of his head that he was leaving the room. Tina knew he was going for help.

Tina shifted her position on one knee and she heard a low sob. She put her arms closer around Peggy and bent her head to hers. There was another sob—then another and another and another. Tina whispered to her.

"It's Tina. You're all right. Just rest here for a while and you can tell me why you feel so awful. As soon as you want to."

The sobbing continued but Tina was thankful none of the convulsive breathing started to indicate hysteria. Tina was not unacquainted with hysteria and she knew how hard it was to stop once it started.

Peggy suddenly found her voice. She murmured, "It's no use. I haven't anyone for me. My mother and father don't speak to each other except in court. The Judge is always in court. Polly dotes on him so much she can't see what's going on. I turn to Dennis and the Judge jumps on me. He is not Dennis. He hates Dennis. He would like to be Dennis. Now he's going to send Dennis home. God knows what will happen to me. I've had enough. I can't cope any more, especially with the Judge. Oh, it's all such a mess!"

Peggy indicated with her body that she wanted to stand up. Tina and Peggy stood up together. Peggy tossed her long ringlets back with a shake of her head and pulled a kleenex out of her pocket with which to wipe her face and eyes.

"I think I hate all of them! All of them—except Dennis and—and maybe Polly. I want to go home. But the Judge is sending Dennis home and keeping me here. He thinks he can do as he pleases but he'll see!"

Tina was relieved to see the American who had helped her reappear in the doorway to the lab. And with him came the Judge, Polly, and what looked like part of an ambulance crew. Peggy immediately let out a shriek and tried to run away. Tina just had time to grab her and hold on. What was presumably the intern or doctor attached to the ambulance advanced quickly. Without asking he grabbed Peggy's arm and inserted the needle he had had hidden behind his back.

The Judge advanced, saying, "She has to have some help."

Tina was in a mood to disagree "I thought I could talk to her. Now she'll just wake up with a headache." The ambulance intern signaled to two of his assistants. They rapidly put together a stretcher and Peggy more or less collapsed on it. They took her away. Oddly enough, no one said anything.

CHAPTER

11

You will spend your first night
on your Nile boat, the Isis II.

Tina was surprised at how she felt. Peggy had gone off in the ambulance with the Judge. The American who had helped had introduced himself as an engineer attached to the temple site. She had thanked him; she could have kissed him but she restrained herself. Peter appeared in a rush and took her in his arms. That was when she began to feel lightheaded. She had never fainted in her life but she felt as if she might. Peter found a chair and made her sit down. The American engineer gently shoved her head down between her knees. Things seemed to fade out and in again.

Hada rushed into the room. "She'll be all right in a minute," said Peter. "She saved Peggy's life. Reactions are funny."

Hada patted the perspiration on her forehead. "We should be thankful she saved her life. I don't know what to think. This is the first time I've ever had such a thing occur." She glanced at Tina. "What an awful experience."

Tina straightened up and started to rise. The American put out his hand to steady her. "Where do you want to go?" he said to Peter. "My car is right outside. I gather you're part of a tour."

"We have to go back to the airport," replied Hada. "After I show the tour the hill construction."

"I'll take you to the airport right now," insisted the American. "Your wife can rest for a bit until the others come."

"She's had a shocking experience," said Peter. Tina was happy she could hear such concern and—pride in his voice.

"She's got guts!" said the American.

And that was what they did. The American drove them to the airport and insisted on having a beer with them. The awful feeling began to go away. They talked. The American's name was Riley and he was actually attached to the Defense Department of the United States. But for some reason which was not at all clear, Riley was an employee of the Egyptian government to monitor United States aid. Tina thought to herself it was a classic conflict of interest but she felt too exhausted to say so. The American left and she and Peter went to sit in the shade outside the building. There was a breeze. Although hot and sandy, it felt good.

They sat quietly. "The ladies room is over there to the right," said Peter.

"Good God," exclaimed Tina. "That was hours ago!"

"Only about thirty-five minutes, I think."

"Excuse me." She found she could laugh. "I'll be right back."

Neither Tina nor Peter was surprised that the tour bus did not show up for close to forty minutes. It was obvious everyone wanted to know what had happened, but even Bette was bashful about asking. They boarded the airplane and Tina promptly went to sleep with her head on Peter's shoulder. Somewhere between Abu Simbel and their destination at Aswan, Peter put his arm around Tina. She awoke as they landed, with her face resting under his ear. Most uncomfortable, but she could smell his shaving lotion. She felt secure.

As she moved, she heard him murmur, "O.K.?"

She straightened up. "I am happy to report I feel much better now. You know I almost fainted?"

"I know you did. Do you want to talk about it now?"

She indicated the tour group around them and slowly shook her head. At that moment the airplane touched down. There was no time to do anything but gather their belongings and get in line.

Off they went in another bus. This time they drove quickly to the shore of the Nile, then along it, until they were on a city street and arrived without delay at a place where boat after boat was tied up to the bank of the river, four and five abreast.

"I'll be darned," exclaimed Peter. "Will you look at that! We are not alone!"

"It looks just like pictures of the Mississippi River. Except the boats don't have side wheels and they're more modern looking." She surveyed the river and the sky. "But, you know, it's sort of beautiful. Look at the white of the boats and the brightly colored flags and the blue sky with that cloud over there."

"For me," commented Peter, "I hope the bed is comfortable. I'm beginning to think I'm tired."

"We're really exhausted. But I won't tell anyone if you don't."

The tour group descended one by one from the bus.

They comprised a definitely rumpled collection of Americans. Obviously Americans. Cameras around their necks. Hawaiian polo shirts. Yellow and red shorts. And Reeboks.

Tina remembered with a kind of internal grin her client who had insisted America had no culture. She had argued for the culture and now she thought she was seeing a part of it. Hit or miss clothing, but comfortable. Expensive equipment from all over the world. Seeming nonchalance but eyes and ears at attention. No one was missing anything. A certain politeness with everyone around them. They were discussing tipping.

Down they all went, perhaps fifty feet, on rather steep stone steps to the level of the boats. John, the trip coordinator, was standing at the gangplank with his clipboard in hand. Tina blinked; she had not expected to see him again so soon.

"Welcome aboard. Welcome aboard. All. We're the last boat through. On the outside." He pointed to his right. "Just pass through the other boats—If you want to buy gifts there is a gift shop on our boat, up one deck—Welcome aboard! The purser will collect your tickets in the salon and the immigration inspectors will take your passports at the same time. Your passports will be returned to you the day before we land."

"There's just one thing they should remember every time," Joe was heard to remark. "We can't get home to the United States without our passports and there's not one of us who doesn't want to go home."

Like the others, dutifully, Peter and Tina crossed through the other boats to the salon of "their" boat. All the interiors looked pretty much the same. Dark wood, polished glass, stainless steel and brass, the floors covered wall to wall with deep carpets. The immigration officers or the customs men, whichever they were, sat behind a long table with what looked like account ledgers open in front of them. They did not smile but stared at those who came before them. Peter turned in their passports and was then told by a white jacketed individual who was standing in the doorway that their stateroom was number 25 on C deck. Peter turned to Tina. He looked angry.

"Do you have the confirmation of our reservations? In your pocketbook?"

The white jacketed individual, who bore on his pocket the label 'Assistant Purser,' responded before Tina could reach into her purse. "We had to change your room from what was originally promised. But your fare will be reduced proportionately."

Peter began to get red in the face. "We're perfectly capable of paying what we reserved. We already have. If I remember correctly, you've given us one deck lower than we paid for. I'd like to see the captain or the tour leader. Now."

The Purser began to lick his lips and grin. "Why you should look at cabin. They are all very much the same. Same size. Same bathroom. Americans very particular about bathrooms. All the same. Just different deck. You see."

Peter looked at Tina. She shrugged. "Let's look," she said.

"All the same. You see."

Miraculously their luggage appeared and off they went down stairs, two decks, following the blue caftan who carried their luggage. He stopped at the door bearing "25" on its face, put down the luggage to the left of the door and inserted the key. Tina and Peter looked in the room eagerly, as the door opened.

"Not so bad," said Tina.

"It couldn't be much smaller," replied Peter. "There's not even a chair to sit on."

"Darling, I don't want to fight any more today. So I'm a coward but I want to lie down."

"I know, I know. But, damn it, they're taking advantage."

"Let me rest until supper, then I'll fight on your side. Dear, I'm sorry."

Peter put his arm around her. "We won't be down here much anyhow and we are saving $350." The blue caftan dumped their luggage in the room and quietly shut the door.

Peter went to the window, not porthole, to look at the Nile. There it was flowing in front of his eyes. Close up. He had expected to see pollution but the water was clean. No silt. No debris. The color of the water was bluish amber. The blue Nile. Peter smiled to himself.

Meanwhile, Tina sat down on the end of the bed. She felt the mattress, then gently lay back with her eyes shut. Peter gave her a long, careful look and went into the bathroom. Quietly, he shut the door.

Tina was awakened just a short time later by Peter rummaging around in their suitcases. "What are you looking for?" she asked sleepily.

"The thermometer," Peter replied. Tina sat up in a hurry.

"Do you think you have a fever? They say everyone gets sick. It's the awful water."

"I'm worried about you," said Peter, as he sat back with the thermometer in hand. "There's something wrong with you. Put this in your mouth." And he handed the thermometer to Tina.

"There's nothing wrong. I'm just tired. I think what I need now is some food." But she did put the thermometer in her mouth.

"So we'll have some very soon. Dinner is at 7:15. But there's something more. You're not yourself at all."

Tina caught Peter by his arm and pulled him down to sit beside her. She snuggled up to him and he rubbed her back.

"I'm so glad I've got you! Just the two of us. We can make it together. Just don't let anything happen to us. I like us just the way we are." She sounded funny with the impediment in her mouth.

"What is that supposed to mean? Hmm?" Peter looked her straight in the eyes, then took away the thermometer and kissed her. Finally he looked at the temperature reading. "Absolutely normal."

Tina looked down at her hands. "Every time I think of it, I can see it over again. It's the way it was when my mother died, I kept seeing how she looked while I waited for the doctor."

"You're talking about Peggy."

"You and I really love to live. We find it interesting. We may get angry or frustrated or depressed, but at the same time we know just around the corner something nice will happen or we'll just like being together—like now—or something funny will happen. There are so many options! But for Peggy, she's just guilty—God knows of what. She wants out."

"What did she say?"

"What she said I don't like. Apparently the Judge is as bad as Dennis." Peter made a sound of surprise and disbelief. "I know. She said the Judge was sending Dennis home to have her for himself. Apparently Polly can see no wrong in her husband—"

"There I would agree," interrupted Peter.

"Quite frankly, it's the kind of law I don't like to practice. You know that. So here it is with me personally involved and on our vacation. It's not fair."

"As you just almost said yourself: Who ever said anything about fairness?"

"Yeah, I know, no one promised us a rose garden. I am so sick of that!"

"Shh! Shh!" Peter smoothed her hair back from her forehead.

"At least I feel better now! You're your old self again!"

"It is disgusting!" Tina swung her feet around, ready to stand up. "That poor kid! That's all she is, just a kid. With two grown men, one who publicly does, or is supposed to, exemplify the moral standards of the community, both engaging in sexual exploitation of the worst kind! Sometimes I think God should have forgotten Noah and sunk the Ark!"

Somewhere in the upper areas of the boat a gong sounded. It was a loud gong.

"Whoops! Dinner." Peter checked his watch. "Just on time."

He stood up and began to rip off his shirt and slacks. The shoe of his left foot caught in his pant leg and he was trying to balance on one foot, hopping around, while he worked his shoe free.

"Sometimes I don't know what you think of me." She stood up more slowly and watched his antics with a grin on her face. "Do I gather you are more interested in food than I am?"

"We both are interested in food and don't pretend. What I meant was that you're off on another attempt to better the world."

Tina went into the bathroom, leaving the door open. "You mean you'd have done nothing when I saw her about to hang herself!"

"Good heavens, no. You go off on these tangents and I certainly have no objection. But this one may be more than we bargain for—or you bargain for. We're dealing with pretty fundamental motivations. We don't really understand exactly what's going on. It could be that Peggy is the one who is unbalanced. It could be the Judge is trying to help her. And it could be he is exactly right about Dennis."

Tina came out of the bathroom in her briefs and bra and dove into the open suitcase. She emerged with a slip and white pumps, then switched to the second suitcase. There she found a lavender dress flecked with gold. In no time she was dressed and putting on her gold necklace and earrings in front of the one mirror in the stateroom. Peter tied his tie standing behind her, then put his cheek against hers so that they both saw their reflections in the mirror together.

"Not bad for five minutes."

"I haven't put on my face yet." She looked at herself more closely in the mirror. "What a mess! I'm beginning to look my age." And she went to work. Peter sat on the bed to change his shoes.

Late, but not too late, they got to dinner. The food was by no means gourmet but quite adequate. All the members of the tour appeared to be hungry and "fell to" with a will. The wine flowed freely with the result that everyone felt revived by the end of the meal. Tina was asked several times what had happened and she replied that Peggy had had an accident. She had just happened to be present. She noted the quick smile on Polly's face as she heard Tina's explanation. The Judge had been too tired to come to dinner but they were taking soup and a sandwich to him in his cabin.

Bette was still worried about Wilbur Mott. She demanded of Hada, "I thought you said Wilbur would join us tonight."

"I talked with the Inspector earlier," replied Hada. "Mr. Mott will take the first plane from Cairo tomorrow morning. He will be here before we sail."

After dinner Tina and Peter joined the Atkinson couple on the top deck. The moon was just rising over the Nile. The two couples stood with their arms around their respective spouses. It was both romantic and beautiful as the golden path came to the side of the boat where they stood. "I wonder if they schedule this on purpose," mused Mr. Atkinson.

"Now I bet you're glad the Ark didn't get sunk," whispered Peter in Tina's ear.

"Something better than that," replied Tina. "I'm glad we're here together, tonight, and that—" she kissed Peter below the ear, her lips hidden in shadows from the Atkinson couple, "my heart still beats a little faster when you touch me."

As if by mutual, expressed consent, the two couples said good night very quietly and went down to their cabins. After Peter closed the door he took off his own coat, then helped Tina, gently alternating a piece of clothing with a kiss. She began to do the same thing until she could not keep from giggling. Peter's response was to be a little rougher. "Don't giggle at me, woman. You're in a very vulnerable situation." His body dominated hers as he moved against her. His lips were now demanding, no longer suppliant.

Tina lay down on the bed and Peter lay with her. She could feel his hands, his cheek against her cheek, his arms around her, his fingers, his lips, his tongue. She responded in her own way.

And she felt again the anguish, the desire within her, rising until she had no control. Together they experienced what they had often sought and not always achieved. And when they moved apart, breathless and momentarily exhausted, Tina could not hold back the comment, "I'll bet you would have made a good Noah. It would be hard to forget you." Peter was asleep.

Somewhere, somehow, as Tina went to sleep, she realized she was suddenly sure that she would have a baby, that this time it would count.

Later Peter awoke. He felt restless and he got out of bed. He noticed Tina was uncovered, so he pulled up the blanket over her and tucked it in carefully. It was getting cold in the cabin. She was very, very dear to him at that moment. He walked carefully to the window to look at the Nile. And he was suddenly certain. He wanted to double up his fist and punch the glass in triumph. But he did not want to awaken Tina. He was sure he would be a father and that his son was at that moment beginning to grow into existence. The Pharaohs, he thought, had sought immortality in stones and statues. He was destined for the simplest immortality. He and Tina had made another human being.

12

*On the fourth day we visit the Aswan Dam
and beautiful Lake Nasser.*

There was a different look about the day. There was no dust. The sky was clear blue and reflected in the Nile. Everything was blue and beautiful and they were about to leave the boat to board another bus. Everyone seemed to be in a jovial mood, looking forward to another sightseeing trip— this time the Aswan Dam.

But there was something tugging away at the insides of the gray haired woman. She simply was not looking forward to seeing another dam. She had just seen one in Texas—water, steel, gates, and bleakness—space all over the place and nothing to break the sameness. Why was she going? She didn't want to miss anything! What a reason. She could have stayed on the boat and enjoyed some solace with a book on the upper deck. But here she was, trailing along after people to view a dam which was supposed to be one of the highlights of Egypt.

She found herself sitting alongside the white haired lady on the bus. Another single on the trip. She felt comfortable in her company. Not because she was another single but because she had her own identity and knew it. The gray haired woman looked over the other members of the tour seated in front of her. One thing this trip had made her realize was that in spite of great strides women had made in the last fifty years it was still a couple oriented society. Neither spouse dared let the other go. Everyone on the tour was a couple except these two women and Mr. Mott. She was trying not to let it affect her.

She was having a difficult time finding herself after a divorce and retirement. She didn't discuss it very much but she wondered what it was she was looking for. Doing things gave one some purpose but she knew that was not the main answer. She knew it was deeper meaning that provided the substance to one's life. Perhaps she'd stumble over it. The key would be to recognize it for its worth. So she dragged along just in case, just in case something might happen.

She started a conversation with her companion and was amazed that they could become deeply absorbed in whatever they were talking about. They seemed to be able to discuss everything from the newest hairdo to African elephants—and enjoy it.

But where was Wilbur Mott? She scanned the heads of the people seated in front of her. Nothing like. She turned to her new friend beside her. "Do you see Wilbur Mott?" She waved her hand. "Or have you seen him this morning?" The white haired lady turned to her with a puzzled look. She continued, "He was supposed to be with us by this time, wasn't he?"

They were interrupted by Hada, who looked charming, doing her bit to provide them with new information about the political background of the Dam. "The Aswan Dam was originally started by the British around 1900, and enlarged several times. It had to be increased in size to make more land in Egypt for farming. The Soviet Union was entrusted with the final project and a High Dam was completed in 1972. The Dam was of massive proportions and the body of water formed by it was named Lake Nasser, after the President of Egypt who was in office at that time."

The gray haired woman was gazing out the window while Hada was speaking. Actually this information was not holding her attention. It was the landscape that interested her. Maybe she'd paint again. Do something that would absorb her total attention while doing it. Painting to her had always meant solitude. She knew that complete solitude needed to be supplemented by human interchange. By love.

She turned toward the white haired lady who seemed very interested in what Hada was saying.

"Did you notice the change in the landscape since we got on the bus?" The white haired lady turned her attention from Hada to the view out the window. "From gentle green to glaring desert sands," mused the gray haired lady. "It reminds one of the illustrations in the Arabian Nights—all blue and gold and pink and violet."

The luminosity of the area was blinding.

"We are coming to the gateway of Africa," responded the white haired lady. "It's where Egypt ends and Africa begins. It used to be called Nubia. Nubia stands for gold and the ancient Nubians grew very wealthy. They are still known today as traders. Supposedly they take great pride in their honesty."

Their attention returned to Hada. "Here we are, coming to the dam—which, as you know, created a problem and flooded some of the most valuable monuments and temples in Egypt. Now it is causing silting. We have no solution to that as yet."

The gray haired woman found that she was more interested in this background information than she thought she'd be. As they approached the Dam they saw a huge modern monument. Hada told them it was a stylized lotus blossom set up in memory of all those who had worked on the Dam.

The parking place where they stopped was not far from the Lotus Blossom Memorial. As they descended the bus steps to get a better look at the Dam, they blinked from the bright blinding sun, seeing nothing but the vastness of the water in front of them. It seemed as if the lake went into infinity. It was massive, reminding the onlookers that that's the way the Egyptians liked to do things—big! Here again the gray haired woman was reminded of Texas. What a strange similarity. The world was shedding its differences one by one. Soon it would be one huge, homogenized world, the difference between countries just a matter of time and distance.

The gray haired woman stretched herself over the railing trying to get some pictures which would record the experience. The sun was shining in the lens of the camera. She refocused. Something was obstructing the view. In her line of vision, there was a strange object bouncing and bobbing and hitting the sides of the dam gate. The thing was covered with what appeared to be seaweed, or a reddish-brown blob of fur hanging off a round ball. It banged two or three times, first in one direction and then another, and then like a baby being pushed out of its mother's womb, the battered object washed through the gate, rolling over and over and down the water-slide. She made an effort to comprehend what she was seeing. She was dumbfounded. Speechless. It had to be a human body.

She quickly changed from her camera to her binoculars and could see a face bashed to a bloody pulp, the eyes open wide as if to see where it was going. A jacket, English tweed, and torn pants dragging behind, as if the body had had a struggle before it arrived in the water. One arm was wound around the head perhaps in an effort to protect it, while the other was nothing but a bloody stump with the forearm missing.

She started to feel sick and screamed out for Hada to come to her side. Hada had been pointing out sites on the other side of the Dam. She stopped in the middle of a sentence, and quickly moved toward the gray haired woman. She gasped, then did not utter a sound. The rest of the group, noticing the ghoulish sight that was part of the scene, started yelling that there was a body in the water.

Hada recovered, and, with a firm but shaky voice, urged people to remain calm and not to move. "I'll call the authorities immediately."

She turned to the gray haired woman, and asked her to be ready to describe what she had seen to the authorities. "I'm sorry. I'm sorry. This is unbelievable!" she exclaimed. "I hope this will not ruin the trip for you." She hurried off.

Meantime, the body was catapulted into the shallows of the Dam where it bobbled and bounced in utter helplessness.

Joe yelled, "I'll jump in."

"No, you won't," Bette blurted in a hurry. "Let the authorities take over."

The gray haired woman felt faint. "I think it's Wilbur Mott," she said.

Death is before me today
Like the fragrance of myrrh.

They all scrambled down the side of the dam toward the shallows, taking rocks and sand with them as they tried to keep their footing. It was not easy. But they could not stay away. They hurried to the bottom in order not to miss anything. They sought to see in actuality the horror they imagined would confront them once they were there. Not that they would gloat over the sight of Mott's mangled body. But it had something to do with wondering why it was Mott—and what happened to him and why they were involved. You could tell by the expressions on the faces of the group it was not something they were looking forward to. Just the same, they pressed on, pushing and shoving one another to make sure they could get as close a look as possible. It would be a picture they would never forget. A picture that would be a part of their conversation for years to come as they remembered their Egyptian trip.

An apprehensive look crossed the face of the gray haired woman as she stumbled toward the shallows to be interrogated by the Inspector. What, if any information could she give that would help? She preferred not to be involved but could not worm out of it. As a retired school teacher of language and literature, she knew the importance of every word uttered and every glance given. She knew she had seen a haunted look on Mott's face way back at the hotel. To her that was important. Yet she feared the Inspector would not listen to such description. It was not factual. She would like to scream in her exasperation "Why am I involved in this at all? I did not want to come to the Dam in the first place."

The gray haired woman knew she looked totally disheveled. She tried to regain her composure as she dug out a Wipe 'n Dri to wash off the sweat pouring down the side of her nose and into the corner of her very dry mouth. She brushed her gray hair off her forehead and found herself wondering whether this was the time in life to give herself a lift by coloring her drab hair. What a strange time to think of that! She would be facing a dead body. She would be trying to come up with black-and-white, yes-and-no answers. The law in her experience did not require the truth, just an answer. She wished she weren't so analytical. She was thinking too much. Instead she should be concentrating on her footing. She was awkwardly sliding in the loose soil underfoot and Joe came up to grab her arm. She was more humiliated than grateful. It had been a long time since anyone had done this for her in a casual way.

"We've got to get you there in one piece. You're the only one who knows the scoop."

She cringed. Tina and Peter stepped forward and without saying a word took their places by her side. They knew how she felt. She glanced over to where her white haired friend stood and received a gesture of encouragement. It gave her a spurt of courage and confidence.

The Inspector took an authoritative step toward his source of information. He cleared his throat to give the cue that he was about to start a very important interview.

"Madame, you must now tell us everything you saw from the very beginning."

"When I first saw Mr. Mott in the hotel—"

"Please, please. I need the facts. When you first saw the body coming through the dam gates. From that beginning."

"But that is not the beginning," she snapped.

"Madame, I need your cooperation. You saw the body first—or did you?"

"My God." His macho attitude collided with her feminist views. She could have spit on his so-called authority. It was obvious his lack of sensitivity utterly limited his perception. Joe yelled, "Shit. Let's get this over with so we can get out of this burning sun. Put this behind us and get on with things." The gray haired lady felt absolutely isolated and winced at his lack of concern.

A helpless look passed over her face again as she answered the Inspector. "Yes, I saw the body or what turned out to be the body."

All the time the Inspector was questioning her, she was distracted by the shocking activities in front of her. A couple of the Inspector's assistants were attempting to remove the body of Mott from the shallows without disturbing it any more than was necessary. The white haired lady was trying to make suggestions but no one listened. For once, Bette was quiet while the others of the group looked steadily at their feet.

The gray haired woman fumed. She had never been so aware of her impotent position before. She rationalized that it was because she was in Egypt but immediately realized that most of the attitudes toward women elsewhere in the world were equally humiliating.

The assistants, with slow, panther-like movements, and the expertise of magicians, carefully slipped a net under the body and gently lifted it out of the shallows onto the wet sand at the edge of the water. The closeness of Mott's mangled body brought embarrassed silence to the group—each thinking his own private thoughts. They looked at the body and they looked at each other. Collectively they were horrified.

Here was Mott. The once stately figure with the trim look of a dandy now looked bloated and colorless with hardly any definable facial features except the eyes—wide open, probing the heavens, reminding one of that peculiar way the Egyptians had of doing the eyes of the mummies—black centers staring out of stark white backgrounds. The eyes practically jumped out of the face. The clothes were in shreds, hanging limp and wet over parts of the body indiscriminately. Had he been alive, he would have been shocked to learn that he was exposed to the world—especially those he had tried so hard to impress. His penis hung limp and flat across the top of his thigh. People tried not to stare, but it was obvious they did. No one attempted to cover the body. Official identification must be made first.

The Inspector turned to the gray haired woman. "Do you recognize this body as that body you saw being washed out of the gates of the dam?"

"I do." Was this a wedding ceremony, a court room scene, a charade—or a dead body? It all had the same ring.

"How would you identify this body by name?"

"His name is Wilbur Mott. I think."

"You think, you think," said the Inspector through clenched teeth. "This is no game. You can't think. You must know. Is it or is it not the body of Wilbur Mott?"

"Yes," said the gray haired woman.

The white haired lady interrupted. "What she means, Inspector, is that the man introduced himself as Wilbur Mott."

"What? What did you say?"

"Yes," said the gray haired woman.

Meanwhile, Bette was looking uneasy as she clung tightly to a clumsy package. She shifted her gaze to the Judge who was standing close by. She pulled him aside as she spoke to him in a low voice.

"Mr. Mott left me this package or at least I guess he did. At least it got mixed up in my packages. It may be valuable. Should I give it to the police?"

The Judge reached for the package without hesitation. His response surprised her. "I'll take it," he said. "Hand it over." As Bette continued to try to hold onto the package, he repeated, "I said, hand it over." And jerked it away.

There was no arguing with the Judge's tone of authority. She quivered as she obeyed, most unlike Bette.

Peter, watching from the distance, noted the unusual display of temper from the Judge. In order to maintain some control on the situation, he decided it was time to do something about covering the body of Mott. He bent over to put the arms in position first.

"Let me help," said the Judge disagreeably, as he jabbed at the body with the end of his crutch. "He needs to be turned over."

Peter watched a very angry cane slam into the thigh of Mott. The flat, dead penis flew up with the jolt. Peter could not restrain the thought that the Judge's action was downright perverse.

Bette screamed as the body moved. Joe took her by the elbow and helped her from the scene. Peter finished covering the body as the Inspector concluded his notes.

The gray haired woman walked away in disgust. She was getting mixed signals from everywhere and could not put them together. The only thing she knew for certain was that they had a mystery on their hands. Was it murder? Was it suicide? Was it an accident?

The group trudged up the hill more slowly than when they had come down. No wiser than before. Hada wondered how they would conjure up the energy to absorb the next site-seeing venture. It was to be Philae, where they would hear about the legend of the gods who put Osiris' body together after it was torn asunder. There was a strange connection between life and death in this land which tried to defy death and preserve life forever. As the gray haired woman was considering these things, the white haired lady caught up with her, put her arm about her waist and said, "Congratulations for hanging in there. I'm proud of you." And she smiled with a knowing look.

14

*Breakfast on board, then, a short ride
to visit the beautiful island temple of Philae.*

The white haired lady did not like what she thought she saw in the set of the Judge's jaw and in the downward twist of Dennis' mouth. She was sitting behind them on the bus, across the aisle, as they started the trip to Philae. She would have said that Dennis was cringing from the Judge and that the Judge had cornered Dennis in his seat. Polly sat directly behind them with all their coats and packages piled between her and the window. She sat rigidly, looking neither to left nor right.

The gray haired woman sat beside the white haired lady. "He—I mean Hakim," said the gray haired woman "is so insensitive. He'll never get anywhere. Mott has been murdered. You can see that. And we don't know whether we're in danger or what."

Hada began to explain over the loudspeaker that Philae was another Egyptian temple complex which had been saved from the waters of the Aswan Dam by being moved to a higher elevation and restored in the new location. The white haired lady noted with alarm that the Judge appeared to be chastising Dennis in spurts; that is, he leaned closer to him, said a few words with great vehemence, then sat back, then repeated the same actions. She could not determine what was being said, but Dennis seemed to curl up his whole body a little more after each onslaught.

The white haired lady had seen too often the effect of intimidation on the bodily responses of the other party. As an attorney trying to retire, at the other end of the spectrum from Tina and Peter, she had little faith left for judges and the so-called judicial system. It came as no surprise to her that whatever was going on between the Judge and Dennis was being handled by the Judge with intimidation, not with reason or reasonableness. According to the theory books, the law and its administrators were supposed to work on logical principles. It seemed to the white haired lady that logic, mercy, and realism had not been heard of recently in the judicial system.

The gray haired woman interrupted her thoughts. "Something is very, very wrong," she said. "I can feel it."

The bus stopped by a docking area and they all got out. The white haired lady looked around her eagerly. She was familiar with boats and this was obviously a commercial area for boats, largely small boats with outboard motors. Hada divided her party into groups of four and stood by while they climbed into their respective boats and took their seats. Dennis managed to shake the Judge and get into a different boat from the Judge and Polly. As the blue caftaned operator (why did they all wear blue?) started the outboard motor, the white haired lady shook her head and had to laugh. He held a lighted cigarette between his fingers and at the same time switched the open gasoline container for the outboard from one side of the boat to the other. She breathed a sigh of relief when he finally got under way. Once she had crossed a lake in Guatemala with a native operator who lit and smoked cigars as he poured gasoline from one open container to another. She had congratulated herself, silently of course, ever since that she must have nine lives like a cat. And here she was using up another one. She was losing count.

They moved out into the lake. The sky was blue and clear; the water was blue and shallow with the result that one could see reeds bending with the flow of the water, low lying rocks and, once in a while, fish as they swam under the boat. Except for the racket of the outboard motors it was a scene from paradise. The white haired lady took a deep breath and exulted. This was more like it.

Hada called out across the water "Look to your left. There is the island upon which the temple complex was originally built." The island was a low lying rock ledge now almost completely submerged by the waters of Lake Nasser. Looking straight ahead, as the boat turned, they saw Philae emerge. It looked like a painting against the sky.

There it stood to the honor of its gods; the tourists were worshippers approaching humbly to do homage. Because this was a temple more recently erected than Abu Simbel it was easier to recognize the various classical parts. Constructed of sandstone grayed by time, etched with purplish green lichen, the temple complex pleased the eye both in its placement on a rocky outcropping and the relationship of its individual parts.

The little outboards floated up, starboard-sides touching an obviously worn and ancient stone quay. As the tour occupants climbed out of the boats they came immediately into a grouping of black, turbaned street salesmen. Their wares were laid out in front of them on tables covered with white cloth. The tables extended up to the temple walls. These were the Nubians—calling, gesturing and laughing, crying out their honesty while jacking up the prices to match the looks of the prospective purchasers.

Peter held out his hand to the white haired lady as she stepped from the boat. "I don't know what else is apt to happen but here we are at the next stop," he said.

The Judge and Polly pushed through the Nubians, went up the slope and into the Temple, then moved quickly to the left. They came to a halt against an outlying wall where there was room to spread out what Polly had been carrying. The Judge was breathless, panting after his exertion. Polly looked at him with concern.

"This trip is not doing you any good."

"Let me worry about that. I'm a big boy now."

"What is that supposed to mean? You couldn't wait to get off by yourself. Now here we are and we haven't even looked at the temple. It's supposed to be one of the most beautiful—" She stopped talking and stared. The Judge had unwrapped one of the parcels she had been carrying. She saw real gold, inlaid with silver and precious stones which dazzled the eye where they reflected the high noon sun. The gold was a mask, a mask of a woman and the silver and gems outlined the features, the eyes, hair and throat. "What is that!" she whispered. "Where did you get that?"

"That nitwit gave it to me."

"Bette? Sometimes I suspect she's anything but a nitwit."

"Mott apparently had placed it with her for safekeeping. She claims she didn't know it but I'll take that with a grain of salt. She's scared now he's been murdered and wants me to turn this over to the authorities!"

"Murdered! Is that what happened?" Polly looked horrified and pulled back from the Judge, the mask and the wall. "You—you didn't do it."

The Judge grimaced and shook his head. "You watch your mouth. This is no game. Hakim is all alert. He is not so bland as he looks."

"Will you tell him?"

"You know me better than that."

"You're going to take it home with you." Her voice rose toward a shriek. "How in the world do you think you'll get that through customs?"

The Judge covered up the mask and wrapped it carefully back in its paper. "The trick here is to keep Hakim from knowing that we have the thing. He knows something is up. Probably he knows the mask is missing and now he knows Mott was in some way involved. He has had no reason to know anyone of us is involved but now he will have his suspicions." He presented the mask package to Polly. "I want you to keep the mask. Obviously I can't handle it and my crutches. If he catches on or searches everyone or something happens so the mask is found—you don't know anything about it. You've mixed up your packages with Bette. We'll let her take the rap. Understand?"

"You really think I am stupid, don't you!" hissed Polly. "Suppose I don't want to be your fall guy. The proper thing to do would be to go to Hakim and let him take care of the thing. For once assume Bette is perfectly straightforward."

"Do you know how much that thing is probably worth? Do you have any idea?"

"I suppose I'd shock you if I said I didn't care. That I'm more interested in your career and reputation, and maybe your future on a higher court. Suppose you get caught. That's it!"

"And suppose I don't get caught! We can ransom this." The Judge's words came out like bullets. Little bubbles of saliva had formed in the corners of his mouth and the force of his speech blew them onto Polly and the packages. "I don't intend to keep it. I know I have no use for it. I'm not a collector and I don't propose to become one. But—" He jabbed out with his finger. "I know two or three collectors. I don't think they'll really care where that beauty came from."

Polly turned aside and looked out over the water. She could hardly believe this conversation was taking place. This was not the first time she had found herself completely unable to understand this man to whom she had been married for twenty-three years. What got into him at times! She feared for him, and there had been times when she feared for herself.

Peter suddenly appeared on the other side of the wall. His camera was out and he took his photograph before either Polly or the Judge could stop him. "Got you that time! Good candid shot." He pulled himself nimbly up over the wall to stand beside them.

The Judge turned to him with a smile. "Wish I were young like that." He pulled out his handkerchief and wiped his lips.

"Beautiful view, beautiful from here."

Polly began to gather up the packages and sweaters. "I'm glad you could rest a little," she said to the Judge.

"Can I help?" asked Peter. "I saw you standing there and I thought that was the trouble. Tina and I admire you for even attempting something like this!"

"Once in a while it gets me," said the Judge, in feigned self-pity. "But most of the time I manage all right. My surgeon was a genius or I'd be in a wheelchair."

"Arthritis?"

"And bone damage."

"Messy. I've had two clients. Industrial accident. So called."

"You can say that again."

The three started off toward the central mall of the temple. One of the sweaters Polly was carrying slipped and fell to the ground. Peter swooped it up before anyone walked on it. "Let me carry the clothing at least," he said. Polly stopped and they adjusted the burdens between them. Polly was careful not to damage the package in which the mask was wrapped.

She looked at the Judge several times. It seemed tears were starting in her eyes. Tina appeared farther down the mall. She was waving her arms to Peter. The two older women were behind her.

"Hada is trying to get permission to go up in the pylon!" she called. "The view is supposed to be terrific."

"How can you get up on those things?" questioned Polly. "They look solid. They must have held up the big temple doors once upon a time."

Peter signalled with his arms and shouted, "With all the bats?" Just at that moment a flight of bats flew out from the right-hand pylon. Tina shrieked and ran toward him. Peter laughed. "I'll bet it stinks in there," he said as Tina came up to them. He put his arms around her and held her for a moment. Hada appeared where Tina had been and signalled all her charges to come. "They won't give permission," she called. The tour group gathered, went back through the pylons, and down through the wall to the quay where the boats awaited them. The Nubians started to shout their wares again. "Three dollar! Three dollar!" Suddenly Hakim, in a police outboard motor, rounded the rocky approach. Two of the Nubians saw him, threw down their wares and ran as hard as they could back through the temple.

Hakim drew his revolver and fired into the air. The boat he was in sidled up to the stone of the quay and two police officers, who had been standing just behind him, leaped ashore and took off after the fleeing Nubians. They were trying to draw their revolvers and run at the same time, as they disappeared into the temple. The tour group stood there and blinked. "What's going on?" shouted Joe.

The remaining Nubians quickly started to pick up their wares and get into boats to which they apparently belonged. Hakim came toward the tour group. "I am sorry if I scared any one. With the gun. They may know something about Mr. Mott's murder. That was no accident."

"They've all closed up and I don't have those bolero jackets for the kids." It was Bette, robbed of her chance to buy just a little more. Several people glared at her. The tour stood on the quay, arms dangling, for a few seconds, then boarded their outboards. The word 'murder' could be heard as a whisper repeated from tourist to tourist.

We visit the Temple of Horus,
the falcon god of Egypt.

The tour group lined up to be placed, two at a time, in seedy looking horse drawn carriages. They were trying to emulate the nineteenth century, but instead looked overused, dusty, and uncomfortable. The horses were not your show horses, or Central Park types, that's for sure. They twitched and swished their tails to keep off mosquitoes and flies—hopefully not the malaria type, since the pills used by most of the group were useless. These insects had fast learned to become immune to man's chemical warfare. Imagine an insect outwitting man. The carriages jiggled up and down, backward and forward, as the impatient horses could not stand the restraint placed on them by their bored looking drivers. The drivers looked at the group with emotionless expressions. The experience of driving tourists up the dusty hill so many times to the

Temple of Horus gave them uncanny insight into human behavior, particularly visitors from other countries.

As Tina started to step into carriage #7, the horse lurched and jolted the carriage sideways causing her to lose her footing. Peter caught her just as she was about to do the split with one foot in the carriage and one on the ground. "Yikes," she cried," Not a very graceful entrance." The driver could not hide a slight smile which played itself out in his eyes, almost imperceptibly.

The horse drawn carriages started up the steep hill, following each other the way parades do in a circus. The town was unattractive; the "hangers on" around the carriages were unattractive; the merchandise was unattractive. Who would be the most vulnerable to the sales pitches? One could feel it coming. And Tina did not feel too enthusiastic about battling the bargainers today. She held Peter's hand and felt good that he was there.

"Someone told me I could buy all my grandkids costumes at the bazaar on the hill." Bette's voice could be heard up and down the hill.

"Guess who?" said Peter. "I wonder if one can become addicted to buying. I never thought about it too much before, but I guess it's possible."

"A bit scary," said Tina. "I wonder if she has any other interests?"

As they approached the top of the hill, they were faced with a moving, yelling, aggressive bunch of salespeople holding out their wares and waving them under people's noses. Bette began to squeal with delight and jumped down from her carriage with the bargaining enthusiasm of a pro.

"We'll never get through the gates of the Temple," groaned Peter. "Want a Coke while we're waiting?"

"I'm staying put and away from that mob, but I'd love something cold to drink." Tina wiped the sweat off her upper lip and straightened her blouse, which had become askew from the jolting ride.

Peter left the carriage and called over his shoulder that he'd be right back. The horse danced. The driver stepped out and left the carriage unattended. Not too secure a feeling, Tina thought. Her feminine breasts sat well in her brightly colored blouse. She felt that she looked attractive today. It was vacation time and it was fun not to have to worry about too much other than how one looked. But this vacation was different. A vacation punctuated with unexplained death and fulfillment in love. It was a lot to think about and put together.

Just as her mind started to wander, her eye caught a disheveled looking female figure striding up the hill. Every inch of her body made a statement of defiance. The female looked very much like Peggy, but Peggy had been left in the hospital. Oh my God. Could it be she? Tina was not close enough to determine this, but watched as the young woman slung her shoulder bag in back of her and shoved her hands in the pockets of her slacks. She could see there were dark circles about the eyes as this person slid behind one of the market stalls and peaked out at the group. Tina looked around impatiently for some sign of Peter. She glanced in all directions but did not see him. Perhaps she should try to go after him. As she started to step out and was concentrating on not upsetting the balance of the carriage, a hand from behind grabbed her on the shoulder. The hand slid down her arm and wrapped itself around her breasts. Peter? Not Peter. A black shiny Cordovan loafer stepped into the carriage and a voice said, "You look lonely. Let me entertain you." She whirled about quickly and snapped, "Get lost, Dennis. Your reputation has preceded you." He laughed, the carriage jolted, he fell on top of her and the horse thinking it was time to go, took off with the two of them, driverless. In the midst of the confusion, they were yelling, and laughing. The driver, running to catch up, hurled himself into the driver's seat. Here she was, on the way to the Horus Temple with Dennis, the two of them together. My God, what next? As they approached the Temple gates, she turned around again to look for Peter, but saw instead, a horrified look on the face of the strange female figure. The figure whirled around and darted down a side alley out of sight.

Hada caught up with the carriage to find out if Tina was all right and she and Dennis jumped to the ground.

The group descended from their carriages to enter the gates of The Temple of Horus, the original falcon god of the sky and

the protector from evil. Dennis managed to stay by Tina's side and to keep up a conversation laced with laughter. One would have thought by all outward appearances that they had been "buddies" and used to this sort of thing. Tina managed to keep the conversation neutral—the weather, the trip itself, Egyptian food, and museums. At the same time she kept looking for the figure of Peggy to appear.

It was not easy to focus on the structure before them, since Horus and the Temple were not exactly in Dennis' line of interest. He salaciously planted his gaze on Tina's breasts, and remarked on her trim figure. She purposely ignored his pointed comments and was determined not to make a scene that would draw attention to this ridiculous "togetherness" which they were sharing.

The sun was blinding. She still could not see Peter. She was dying of thirst and confusion. And she had wanted to concentrate on the history of this, one of the most important gods of Egypt. There must be an extremely important connection between this falcon and all the religious beliefs of Egypt.

Hada, as always the efficient tour guide, waited for her charges to gather close to her. The heat and the dust seemed to be taking its toll on her as well as the tour members. She moved her tongue across her lips to wet them as she explained that Horus was one of the most powerful gods of Egypt and was equated with the pharaoh. Not only did he have the power to protect his believers from evil, but he was the one who led the dead into heaven. Tina stared at the statue of Horus guarding the entrance to the Temple and could not suppress the thought that this strange looking representation of a falcon, with its cocky look and puffed out chest might start to dance like Jimmy Cagney at any moment. The bird was short and stocky, but exuded a kind of vivacity uncommon in all the other gods. She could see that Horus had appeal to the average person. She wished she could share her thoughts with Peter.

"What does this have that the Bronx Zoo doesn't have?" Dennis tried to whisper into her ear with his smart-alec sneer. Tina jerked her head away in disgust.

Hada continued her commentary as they moved into the dark and cool Temple. "The eyes of Horus represented the sun and the moon, and warded off all evil spirits afraid of the light. The myth tells how, at one time, Horus lost his 'moon eye' in a battle with his bad uncle Seth, and then recovered it. It was presented to his father Osiris which helped him regain life. Thereafter the eye of Horus became the center piece of every ceremony of offering."

Tina thought to herself that the dualistic world view of Egypt—with its concentration on the conflict between good and evil, the mysteries of life and death, was not unlike the world of her career. There she grappled every day with the gray areas of things. It would be easy if answers or questions could be checked off as true or false. As she was musing on the subject, her eye caught a dark shadow of a figure moving toward her and Dennis. The figure took its place on the free side of Dennis and slipped an arm through his.

"Hi, Dennis."

Dennis seemed to jump a foot in the air. "Jesus, Peggy. You scared the Hell out of me. I thought you were in the hospital."

"I walked out. After all, how could I keep tabs on all of you in the hospital."

"Oh my God. Wait till the Judge hears this. Peggy, get out of here and let the Judge know where you are."

Tina, meantime, recovered herself enough to move toward Peggy with an outstretched arm, to give her some support. Peggy snapped at her and hissed out with, "Don't you come near me, you snake. How many fields do you play, anyway?"

"Peggy, you've got it all wrong."

Peggy's face was covered with tears as she spit out in front of the whole group, "I can't trust anyone any more. Not the Judge, not Dennis and least of all Dennis' new playmate, Tina."

Tina was speechless. How could she explain? Peggy turned and the echo of her running footsteps reverberated throughout the Temple of Horus. Tina screamed inside for Peter to please come. Meanwhile Dennis automatically put his arm around her shoulder in what she thought could indicate a semblance of understanding.

"No you don't, you bastard!" Peter had appeared.

Tina cringed. It was Peter with the loudest, strongest, angriest voice she had ever heard coming out of his mouth. She dared not look. She heard a Coke can slam against the wall of the Temple as he lunged toward Dennis and grabbed him by his collar—the pink ruffled collar that was Dennis' pride and joy. Riiiiip! As the collar came off in Peter's hand, his face turned a blustery red, and his eyes darted fire as he yelled, "Keep your paws off Tina or I'll mop up the Temple of Horus with you. You've caused enough trouble around here and you're not going to get Tina into the act."

Tina smiled a thank-you to Peter, but he turned on her and between clenched teeth sputtered, "We'll discuss this later."

Hada, at her wit's end, quietly but firmly demanded that they leave the Temple immediately. "This is sacrilege to the god Horus, whose house this is."

Dennis did not attempt to follow Tina. The group silently stepped out into the blinding sunlight and slowly walked through the Temple gates to the waiting carriages. The glances at Peter and Tina were surprised but not critical.

And there was Bette at the merchandise booth decked out with all the layers of Egyptians skirts, blouses, and jewelry that her little, fat body would hold. Obviously she had elected not to go into the Temple of Horus. She chattered gleefully with one salesperson after the other. She was in her glory with all the attention her purchases were creating. Joe stood to one side, reading an advertisement about a circus.

Tina and Peter, not speaking, looked for carriage #7. On the way, they became aware of an angry conversation. They remembered that the Judge had opted to stay outside in his carriage instead of going into the Temple. As they passed him they saw that his strong hands were clenching Peggy's arm and holding her hostage. With steely blue eyes, he coldly demanded that she get into the carriage immediately to go back to the boat with him and Polly. Peggy went limp and showed no semblance of the defiance she'd shown before. As

Polly approached the carriage to get in, she took in the scene in a glance, and stiffened. She said nothing, but one could see her upper lip quiver. All three, Polly, Peggy, and the Judge, squeezed together in one carriage. An incendiary situation, thought Tina.

The drivers lined up their horses. They gave the signal to move and the carriages paraded off, down the dusty hill, toward the boat. The tour group was weary and silent. Tina wondered how all this would ever be resolved. As the carriage in which she and Peter were riding passed that of the Judge, she was shocked to see actual fear in Polly's face.

CHAPTER

16

Overnight in Esna.

S he lay back against the bed pillows and watched as Dennis took off his coat, then his tie, and then his shirt. Peggy had been expecting him to come. The awful trip in the carriage back to the boat was fading away. He did not wear any T-shirt so there was nothing to cover his muscular upper body. He was not a big man in height or otherwise. Just nice. Peggy liked to look at him and she sensed he did not object to being admired. At the same time she felt guilty about her feelings toward him. She had looked up the word "incest" and knew first cousins were not supposed to be in love with each other.

As if he could read her mind, Dennis came over to her and sat beside her on the bed. "Don't look so serious. You look twice your age right now. You're with me, you're not in the hospital anymore."

"I'd like it better if I were twice my age."

"You're just fine the way you are." He stroked her cheek and her neck. "We have something very special. It may never happen to either of us ever again. It doesn't matter what relation we have to each other. We're not planning to have any children." He laughed lightly. "The Judge would kill me!"

"Be careful, Dennis. The Judge is a powerful man."

"Do you know what that means or have you just heard people say that of the Judge?"

"I've heard Polly say it."

"He is powerful but that need have nothing to do with us. We'll have to wait a couple of years and then maybe we'll get married. How does that sound?"

"Are you kidding, Dennis?"

"Well, there might be a problem—since we're cousins, you know. But let's not worry about that now. There are more important things on my mind." He ran his forefinger up her leg.

"Oh, Dennis, it tickles!"

"I'm going to be a big success. And you know what? I'm going to get my business school degree so I can start other branches for my store. You need training and know-how to do that."

"But are you serious about marriage?"

"Oh, you of little faith," laughed Dennis.

He took off his shoes and placed them neatly, side by side, on the floor in front of him. Then his socks. And finally slipped out of his pants.

"Dennis, I asked you a question."

"Don't you know I love you? That's what's important."

"You're just trying to get what you want, aren't you?"

Dennis pushed back her unruly, black curls. "Your hair excites me. You're a senorita and I'm a bull fighter." He plunged his head between her breasts.

"Oh, Dennis, say some more!"

As he removed his shorts and knelt on the bed, Dennis frowned. "Jesus, Peggy, what have you got on. Come on, let's have a little cooperation here."

"Don't you like it?" teased Peggy.

She pulled out her T-shirt to demonstrate its historic declaration "Save the Titanic." The super big one-sized T-shirt displayed the bobbing, sinking Titanic, heaving in purple on her bosom. Dennis ran his hand across her breasts.

"Oh, Dennis, you thrill me every time you come near me—but I hope no one ever finds us! It makes me so scared."

He removed the offending T-shirt. "Relax. Don't worry, kid. Just enjoy it!"

After a few minutes, Dennis reached over and turned on the alarm of Peggy's clock, setting it at two o'clock in the morning. That way he eliminated the danger of oversleeping and being found in Peggy's bed.

Ultimately the alarm went off at two, awakening them with a start. Dennis sat up immediately, swung his legs over the side of the bed, and reached for his pants. He pulled a pack of cigarettes out of a pocket, then looked around for the matches. The room was dimly lighted by reflected moonlight which fell across Peggy's uncovered body. She turned, noted he was looking for something and asked, "What do you want?"

"Matches, what did I do with my matches?" He picked up his pants again to search in the other pockets.

Peggy whispered, "You don't have to go yet, do you Dennis?"

"You know, I've gotta get the hell out of here."

At that moment they both turned toward the door to the cabin, which was opening slowly. The light of the passageway exposed their naked bodies. Dennis had the presence of mind quickly to pull on his pants. The light of the passageway also exposed the outline of the figure of the Judge. Peggy half screamed. Dennis turned on the lamp by the bed. They both could see that the Judge was unclothed, his bathrobe drooped over his shoulders, his body fully revealed.

"What the Hell—" began Dennis.

The Judge interrupted him with a roar. "I knew it!" He lowered his voice. "I knew it! You bastard! Who do you think you are?"

Dennis calmly reached over and picked up his shirt. As he began to button it up, he laughed. "Huh! The pot calling the kettle black." He frowned and flicked the covers up over Peggy. He said to her "You know, I never would have thought this of you. What are you, fifteen? Christ, watch yourself! What will you be at twenty?"

Peggy began to sob. All she could manage to say was "No. No. No." Neither Dennis nor the Judge moved an inch to comfort her.

Seemingly without concern, Dennis completed dressing, put on his shoes and socks and stuffed his shorts into his pocket.

The Judge stood by the door. He held his bathrobe modestly around his body. Dennis left the room but as he passed the Judge, who moved out of the way, he said with a toss of his head, "I guess I won't worry about your threats any more." The Judge opened his mouth and closed it. He made no response to the taunt.

Peggy sat up in bed, wrapping the bedclothes around her. Her voice was unsteady as she commanded, "Get out! Get out of my room!"

The Judge turned his back and with shoulders bent, started to leave the cabin. He limped badly without his crutches. He had to hold onto the door jamb for support. He looked pathetic, his romantic facade completely shattered. For a fleeting moment Peggy wanted to go to his aid. The Judge shut the door between them.

Peggy pulled the twisted covers up around her and sought to hide her head under the pillows. It didn't work. In seconds she was standing on her feet, putting on her night shirt. She had to talk to someone; she couldn't stand it anymore.

She put on her blue, terrycloth robe and left the room. She knew Tina and Peter had the cabin opposite her. She knocked quietly on the door; then, as no one answered, more insistently.

Suddenly the door opened and Peter's half asleep face appeared. "Wha—Peggy! What's going on? What time is it? What's wrong?"

"Oh, Peter, I'm sorry. You don't know what's happened. I've got to talk to Tina."

"It's the middle of the night. Tina's asleep."

"She was asleep but not now." The light in the cabin came on and Tina appeared in her nightgown, sliding her arms into a richly embroidered kimono. She put her arm around Peggy's shoulder and brought her into the cabin. Peter shut the door.

Tina sat down beside Peggy on the bed. "Now, what has happened? What's the trouble?"

"I'm not a whore, am I? Dennis as much as said I was a whore. He said I was only fifteen and by the time I was twenty—"

Tina smoothed her hair and made comforting sounds. "You know that's not true. Dennis knows that's not true."

"But he thinks I sleep with the Judge, too. Because the Judge came in when Dennis was there. And he was all undressed."

"What the hell do you mean?" interrupted Peter. "The Judge?"

"He never came before," insisted Peggy. "I swear it!"

"God, what a mess!" exclaimed Peter.

"I can't go on like this!" Peggy turned on Tina. "You stopped me at Abu Simbel. But you were wrong. I can't go on." Her voice dwindled out on a whimper. She sat with her hands locked between her knees, on the side of the bed. She did not even cry.

Tina looked up at Peter, then rose. She took several steps away. "Peggy," she finally said "I'm going to call your mother and ask her to come get you."

Peggy looked up in horror. "Oh, no! Don't do that! You don't understand. She worships the Judge. She'd never believe such a thing of him."

"But there's Dennis, too. She'd believe the worst about Dennis, wouldn't she? You could go home."

Peggy just shook her head and covered her face with her hands as if to hide. "Let me go kill myself. Let me go. I'm no good. I never was any good. Can't you see? That's what my mother thinks. That's what my father thinks. They can't stand me."

Tina sat down beside her again. "Calm down, Peggy. That's no way to talk. It's the middle of the night. Things always look worse in the middle of the night." Tina paused, then turned to Peter. "I'll tell you what. You go sleep in Peggy's room and Peggy can stay with me."

"I knew it. I just knew it." Peter was half laughing but serious at the same time. "No way! I'll go sleep up in the lounge. I thought I saw this coming." He picked up his bathrobe from the bed and put it on. He opened the door to leave. "See you in the morning, as they say."

"I'm sorry," said Tina.

"I know. I know." Peter shut the door and presumably did what he had said he would do.

To Tina's horror, Peggy sat on the side of the bed staring into space. Slowly she began to suck her thumb.

CHAPTER

17

We visit the West Bank at Luxor, the Valley of
the Kings, the Valley of the Queens . . .

One thing can be said about a tour: there is no time to
think as one day flows rapidly into the next. Everyone
was expected to keep up and everyone did.

The tour bus had stopped for more shopping at an
alabaster factory on the outskirts of the Valley of the Kings.
While some remained in the bus, anxious to go to the first of
the excavated tombs, a few went into the shop for another
round of buying. Bette was, of course, of that group.

Bette had never seen so many pieces of translucent
alabaster. She thought they were beautiful. And in so many
shapes and sizes. She could have bought each one from the
shopkeeper in front of her.

Joe said, "For Christ's sake Bette. We don't have any room."

"But they're so light, Joe!"

"Twenty-five, lady. Just twenty-five. Many many more dollars in New York!" exclaimed the shopkeeper.

"Woolworth's has it cheaper," muttered Joe.

"But these are prettier." Bette held an almost transparent bowl to the light. The light made the alabaster appear silky and shimmering as Bette turned the bowl in her hand. Blurred colors and strange shapes were reflected in the bowl. And beyond the bowl she noted Polly's face peering out of the bus window. She looked weary and concerned and at the same time envious of Bette's enthusiasm. She definitely was not having any fun. Bette felt sorry for her—for a moment—until her mind went on to other things.

She almost immediately found a lovely necklace for herself. She held it up for Polly to see, saying "Come down and have a look. There are really some nice things here!" Polly attempted a half hearted smile and closed her eyes.

Bette turned and found Joe beside her. She commented to him, "Polly has spent this entire trip being concerned about the Judge. And now she's concerned about Peggy as well. It's her turn to have some fun. I wonder what kind of man he is to expect such self sacrifice." She scanned what she could of the group but did not see the Judge. "He must be living in the dark ages."

Joe patted her arm. "You know, Bette, you can't be mother to the whole world."

Bette gave her purchases to the salesman to wrap and went back to the bus. While Joe paid for the purchases, Bette sidled down the aisle of the bus and tripped over the foot of the white haired lady before plopping down beside Polly.

"O.K. if I sit here?"

Polly twisted in her seat. "I don't know where the Judge has got to. He was sitting beside me. I wish he weren't so tired."

"I've noticed that! Do you know if he's talked with Inspector Hakim about the package I gave him?"

"What package? Do I know about a package?"

Bette took a chance. "I mean the package with the golden mask."

Polly almost gasped. "The mask! Isn't that a beautiful thing? Have you ever seen anything like it?"

Bette's heart jumped. "The Judge still has it?"

"I suppose so." Polly looked puzzled. "It belonged to him, he said."

Bette gulped. Now what was she supposed to do?

At that moment the Judge's sunburned, balding head appeared outside the bus, just below where they were sitting. He was followed by Peggy.

Polly at once exclaimed, with relief, "Oh, there he is. I'm so glad. He's back and he looks happier."

They waited while the Judge pulled himself up onto the bus. He came to stand beside Bette in the aisle. Peggy, thankfully, seated herself at the front of the bus. The Judge leaned over and placed a small box in Polly's hand. "To indicate how I feel."

Bette looked quickly to see if he was serious or not.

While Polly opened the box, the bus started up. The Judge had to sit down quickly in a seat three rows behind them.

Polly was ecstatic over the contents of the box. It was a copper cartouche engraved with Egyptian glyphs. Behind them the Judge leaned forward. "It says 'Polly' in Egyptian."

"Is a cartouche good luck or bad luck?" asked Bette.

"Good luck, of course," said the gray haired woman who was sitting across the aisle.

"We haven't had much good luck so far," chimed in the white haired lady.

The bus continued along a descending road through the most forbidding landscape Bette had ever seen. She thought of Death Valley but that was uplifting compared with this sand hill. Sand hill after sand hill. Mountains made of sand and more sand. Some dirty gravel. Of all the depressing environments she had ever experienced this had to be the worst. No wonder they buried people here. It felt like death.

The bus stopped by a sentry box and tickets were handed over to the caftan clad guard on duty. The bus driver opened the door again and the tour members moved out, pushing back their sunglasses and rearranging their cameras around their necks. Hada gathered the group together at the side of the bus, then they entered the tomb.

One by one, the group moved past the two guards at the narrow entrance to the tomb. The wooden walkway was clean despite the tourists, and the sandy floor upon which it was laid was free of litter and debris. As the group passed, another man came up to the entrance carrying a can of some material which was marked with Egyptian letters and a skull and crossbones.

He put it down by the feet of the seated guard and lit a cigarette. After a brief comment in Arabic both men began to laugh.

Bette marveled at the scene before her. She gripped Joe's arm and swept her hands around to indicate the walls covered by patchy brilliant paintings. Osiris and Horus held out hands to the Pharaoh who was buried here. Bette spoke in a whisper as if the dead might hear her. "Are we going to heaven or hell? Joe, you know I have claustrophobia. I don't care how impressive it is. Let's get the hell out of here. I can hardly breathe."

"There's no choice. Nothing out there but hot sun and no shade. Nothing to buy." Joe grinned slightly, mischievously.

At this point, Inspector Hakim pushed by Bette and Joe to go to the head of the group, which by this time was standing around Hada. He stopped by her and spoke quietly, jingling the coins in his pocket. The tour could not overhear, but Hada suddenly looked frightened and angry. She started to deny, then shook her head.

Joe's eyes narrowed. "Hakim's keeping a mighty close look at us all of a sudden. He's warning Hada about someone or something."

Tina and Peter had dropped behind the others to inspect a grouping of gods on the right wall of the tomb entrance. "The colors are really marvelously preserved!" exclaimed Tina.

"For thousands of years there was no air, no moisture, no pollution. There was nothing to destroy the original painting," responded Peter. "Just look at the strength of those colors! I can't take my eyes away from those reds and blues. But boy, what I wouldn't give for a Coke to unglue my mouth. I haven't felt this dry on the whole trip."

There was a crash from the rear of the group, near the entrance, as something metallic banged and clattered against other metal. Peter and Tina hurried to catch up with the others. The walkway descended steeply until actual steps led down even farther. At the bottom of the steps was a small room to the right, lighted but without any paintings or decorations. Hada had entered this room and was addressing the group from the back wall. "Strange things have happened in this room. There are those, you know, who insist that this tomb is cursed. They point to all those who have died after working here or even after working with artifacts which have come from the tomb. The cause of the deaths has not been scientifically proven."

Bette whispered to Peggy, "This is creepy."

As Hada continued, she stepped forward and led the group farther down the wooden walkway into the depths of the tomb. "Some believers have attempted to exorcise the curse. Others believe that this is impossible."

Tina and Peter finally caught up with the group, in time to hear Joe say, "I don't believe in ghosts, but there was a haunted house in the block behind where I lived that we were afraid to play in. Weird things always happened there. We never knew why."

The group made a right turn and continued on. The gray haired woman commented to the white haired lady, "What a lot of nonsense."

"Oh, I don't think so," replied the white haired lady. "We like to think of curses as mere superstition but even today we are sufficiently uncertain to deny their existence totally."

Peter, overhearing the conversation, snorted, lawyerlike, and took Tina by the arm. "Come back here a minute, Tina. I want to show you something." He led the way back, around the corner, where, suddenly, the light at the entrance was once again visible. A noise as of light metal striking rock came from the room where they had previously stopped. The voice of Dennis, low and nasty came to their ears. "Try to strike me once more and you'll never try it again. I'll confiscate your crutchy weapon and that will be that. You use your crippleness to dominate Polly and you intimidate people in handcuffs during the day. You even got to me to do your dirty work. Don't you try to hurt me or Peggy anymore."

There was silence for several moments. Peter had started forward when the Judge's voice interrupted.

"You appear to forget I know a few things about you that you don't know I know. I have always gone on the theory that Polly would not like to see you in jail. I can put you there, you bastard."

"Intimidation, always intimidation." Dennis' voice sneered.

"You bet," retorted the Judge. "Nothing like it!" His voice seemed to be laughing.

"How you got your hands on the Fayum mask I'll never know—"

"Sheer genius," quipped the Judge. He whispered, "Bette gave it to me." His laugh was self-satisfied.

"You don't want me to tell Hakim, do you?"

There was no answer from the Judge.

"I don't have to, you know. How are you planning to get your money out? Ransom?"

There was more silence.

"I thought so. For thirty percent you won't hear anything more from me."

The Judge's voice pierced the silence. "Not a cent is going into your pocket." His voice sounded as if it were muffled by anger. "This is mine. I thought of it in the first place. Mott is dead and you're not going to profit."

"Mott's another thing." said Dennis. "Who did him in? You didn't—"

They all heard footsteps approaching. Peter pulled Tina back and hurried to turn the corner. The approaching footsteps belonged to a workman who swung by them carrying a pail of rags and several cans of cleaning material.

"Well, well, well," said Peter as he pushed Tina toward the light and fresh air at the entrance. "Good for bad rats, I'd say."

18

At the Tomb of the Nobleman.

Polly stood in the sun, and the blowing sand and the sun weighed upon her head and shoulders. It was so hot and so dry she was not even sweating.

Polly had been born in Baltimore, Maryland. She had been born hating the heat and her hatred had never changed. It was hot! She wanted a drink and so did everyone else. The refreshment stand was well stocked with Coke but the owner was slower than slow. Polly saw the Judge buy a Coke and a little while later give it to Dennis—with a smile and some comment. She felt hurt that the Judge had not brought the drink to her.

She went to the stand and bought her own Coke. Peter Carson opened it for her. They had bottles here at the Valley of the Kings, not cans. Hada stood beside her, quenching her thirst with an orange concoction.

"Do you feel any better?" asked Polly. "You seem stuffed up, the way my children get with a cold."

"I'm fine," answered Hada. "When I get home tomorrow, I'll be all right."

Polly looked around for the Judge, as she always did, and found him talking with Inspector Hakim. She could imagine their conversation. All about criminal activities and sociological theories of sentencing. All those things she had studied in college and forgotten as caring for the children took over her life.

She stood sipping her Coke. It dribbled a little down her chin, as it always did. She disliked drinking from bottles anyway. She looked for the Judge again. He was standing looking up at the mountains into which the tombs had been tunneled.

She put aside the Coke bottle and started toward him.

Standing by the entrance to the tomb the group would enter next, the gray haired woman and the white haired lady surveyed the scene before them: the mountains, the sand, the busses, the Coke stand, their fellow tour members quenching their thirsts.

The white haired lady was studying the Judge. "I seldom trust judges and that one is no exception," said the white haired lady.

"Why do you say that? I'm surprised."

"I would say he is politically astute but seems to be the type of ambitious jurist one finds too often today. He has no thought for his wife and his concern for Peggy is pure irritation because she refuses to jump to his every whim. He consumes power like an ice cream cone—I shouldn't be criticizing our fellow tourist. Not that you're even interested."

She studied the gray haired woman for a moment. "Are you getting out of the trip what you thought you would?"

"More than I ever dreamed." The gray haired woman half laughed. She pushed back her exactly combed hair. "In all directions. I have learned that truth is reality but has to be recognized before it can be accepted." The gray haired woman threw up her hands. "What I really mean is—I didn't have the guts to be myself. When I say good-bye at the end of this trip, I will not have lost anything; I will have gained knowledge of myself. And it's been more informative than I thought it would be. That's what you really asked, isn't it?"

Polly caught up with the Judge just as he stepped behind Hada to enter the second tomb.

"I thought you weren't going into any more tombs. The wooden walkway was so difficult with your crutches."

"I have to make the effort. These tombs are too famous to miss."

Polly took the Judge's arm to steady him if necessary and they followed Hada down the walkway. On either side the more than life-size figures of the dead nobleman and his attendant gods gave the tomb the unerring Egyptian identity everyone expected. Peggy followed along with Tina and behind them Bette and Joe. Dennis was in the middle of the line. Peggy looked around once at Dennis as he took another swig of his Coke. He was perspiring profusely. Tina, turning, wondered if he was suffering from a touch of the sun.

Tina said to Peggy, "Is he all right? Or do you care?"

Peggy frowned, "I'm not supposed to care but I do care. Dennis really is a nice, kind guy. The Judge just hates his guts." She slowed her stride to be more confidentially close to Tina. "He's younger and very successful for his age. The Judge wants to boss him around and Dennis won't be bossed. And I guess the Judge thinks he's in competition with him. I never even realized it." She bit her lower lip. "I hope Polly doesn't know. It would hurt her and I don't want to do that."

"That's one way of looking at it," said Tina.

At the head of the line, Hada began with her commentary. She turned to address the group. The Judge, with Polly by his side, stood behind her. "Now, here we have the latest tomb discovery. Contrary to Thutmose, you will note the difference in technique—"

She was interrupted by the sound of Dennis vomiting. He sank to one knee, then stood up and tried unsuccessfully to smile.

"I'm sick," he said. "I'm sorry but I feel awful." He turned to walk back to the entrance, fell against the railing at the side of the walkway, then collapsed in a heap half on the walkway and half on the sand beside it. Peggy gasped and turned to look at the Judge. Joe pushed Bette aside and knelt beside Dennis' body. After a second or two he looked up in total consternation. "Is anyone a nurse even? I don't think he's breathing any more."

Hada pushed her way through the group to Dennis. "I don't believe this can be happening. Where is Inspector Hakim? Go get him. Someone go get him. Please!"

At the other end of the line, someone raced along the walkway to the entrance. His shout could be heard but what he said was incoherent.

Peter put his arm around Tina's shoulder and spoke in her ear. "This is incredible. Two people dead! What is going on? Christ!"

Before Tina could answer, Joe lurched toward them. "I've never been that close to a dead body before. It's awful. He stinks—already."

"It must be poison," said Peter. "I did some criminal work years ago. Poison usually shows up by the way it smells. Not always, but mostly."

Bette crowded into the group. "I want to get out of here! I'm scared. What's going on? Who's going to be next?"

"How could he be poisoned?" questioned Tina.

"We don't know that he was. I was only guessing," quickly interjected Peter.

"Your guesses are usually pretty good," said Tina.

Hakim showed up hurrying from the tomb entrance.

"I'd say we're keeping him busy!" muttered Peter.

Polly had both hands holding onto the Judge's arm. "This is incredible. How can we ever explain things to your sister! What could have happened?"

"His nightly jaunts caught up with him, that's all. Irate husbands in these countries have no patience."

"That's mean," said Polly. "I don't believe it at all."

Inspector Hakim stood up from having knelt by the body. "He's dead. My guess is he was poisoned. Arsenic." He glanced at the Judge.

He turned then, waved at someone who had followed him into the tomb, and issued some orders in Arabic. "We'll get an ambulance as soon as we can." He stepped to the side to speak to the Judge. "He was your nephew, I believe. You will have to identify him."

"Of course."

Peggy suddenly broke into the discussion. "How can you! How can you!" she cried hysterically. "He's dead! Someone killed him! And all you can do is talk procedures. It's like in the movies, old movies on television. It's Dennis! Dennis!"

Polly put her arms around Peggy. "We know. We understand." Peggy pushed her aside and attempted to move through the gathered people to Dennis. Tina, then Peter stopped her.

"You really don't want to," said Peter. Peggy jerked aside and turned her back on the others. She held onto the railing and began to sob.

"Oh, God!" she started. "I don't care what god. This place is full of gods and death. Please make this into a bad dream. I am having a bad dream—" Tina turned at that point with a very worried frown on her face. She looked to Polly but Polly was looking beyond to Dennis' body. Peggy continued, "Dennis, I loved you." Her voice was very low. "You were the first man I loved. I ask the God to take care of you now that I can't. Please, please, someone—" Her voice rose and she turned to the others. "Can't someone cover him up? At least cover him up! He can't protect himself any more."

Everyone in the tour group held still for a moment. Mrs. Atkinson had a scarf around her neck. She started to take it off but stopped. The scarf would have been quite inappropriate. No one had anything, appropriate or inappropriate. When they had dressed, it had simply been too hot for any but their immediate clothing.

Polly tried to think what to do. She knew she had to do something for Peggy. She looked to the Judge for leadership, as usual, but he would not show any concern. She tried to reach Peggy again, to comfort her, but the Judge and Tina and Peter were all in the way.

Peggy wiped her hand across her eyes. "You are all gods here. Isis and Osiris and Horus and all the others. You can help me. You can find the man who did this! He died of poison. Someone killed him. Someone killed him deliberately. I want that man to die, also. I want him dead, too." Her voice was lowered. "Do it for me! You are close here! I see you all around me—"

Polly shoved her way to Peggy. She put her hand gently across her mouth. "You don't know what you're saying! This is crazy talk—" At that moment the men arrived with a stretcher to pick up the body of Dennis. Everyone watched; if one listened carefully everyone sighed a little. The Judge pulled a stick of gum from his pocket, took off the wrapper, and folded the gum into his mouth.

19

For Room Service dial 31.

The Judge was dreaming. He dreamed a nightmare. His heart was beating rapidly. His breath seemed to be labored. He was frightened, scared in his dream. He was being chased by his chief bailiff, Joe Frank. Joe had been with him for six or seven years. They liked each other. Joe was a good guy. Honest, fair, considerate. All the mothers and wives of criminal defendants liked him because he seemed to take a personal interest. It was laughable that he was scared of Joe. But he was. He awoke. There was perspiration on his brow. He looked for Polly, then remembered she had gone to the bazaar with Bette and he had said he would take a nap.

His mind turned to Dennis, where his thoughts had so often been in these last few days. He intentionally shifted his mind. That was over.

He slowly pulled himself up to his feet and grabbed his crutches, which were leaning beside his armchair while he slept. Tina and Peter Carson were coming to dine with him and Polly at seven. Polly had left it to him to order dinner from room service. He guessed he should get the order in to the kitchen. But first he mused on Tina. She undoubtedly would be a mature lover. A very attractive woman, he thought. He could picture her in his arms—feel her smooth skin on his naked body. Sophisticated and warm. Not immature like Peggy! The thought made him writhe inwardly. Not only had she refused his advances; she actually seemed to be repelled by him. He never took rejection easily. How could he have been such a fool to go to her room—undressed and expectant. At least he was rid of her now. With Dennis gone, Peggy had made no more objections to going home. She had left with his brother's wife this morning. Thelma flew over from New York immediately upon hearing that Dennis had been murdered. He had prevailed upon her to take Peggy back with her the same day, rather than stay during the criminal investigation in Egypt.

The Judge straightened his body in the middle of the room, leaning heavily on the crutches. His back always hurt when he was stationary too long. He glanced at his watch and decided he had enough time to look at the mask again. His heart beat a little faster. It was the most beautiful thing he had ever seen. And it was his! He did not want even Polly to share his pleasure.

He went to the straight chair by the window and turned it upside down. The bottom was torn and he had stuck a piece of tape along the tear in the cloth to make a hiding place for the mask. He pulled off the tape and eased out the mask. The mask rested in his outstretched hands, glinting in the afternoon sun. He looked closely at the face drawn on the gold and thought that the ancient artisan must have excelled at his craft. He wondered at the identity of the owners of the mask, first when it was originally made and then as it passed from hand to hand over the centuries. The mask was to him the symbol of wealth and attainment. It was something he had never thought he would have the opportunity to hold in his hands as his very own.

He held the mask in front of his face, then walked to the mirror behind the desk and held the mask beside his face. He examined carefully the dimmed-by-years lines on the face of the mask. The eyes were almond shaped, as he had noticed on the faces of some pharaohs, but it was impossible to tell whether the face was that of a woman or a man. Slowly he limped back to the upturned chair and started to replace the mask. At that moment he heard someone at the door, fitting a key into the keyhole. He attempted to hurry and dropped the mask. Polly let herself into the room.

Polly looked at him oddly. He picked up the mask and replaced it in the covering of the bottom of the chair.

"So that's where you hide it. What I can't understand is how you think you can get it out of Egypt, let alone through American customs." She shoved her clenched fists into the pockets of her skirt. "Roger, security has x-ray detectors. Anything metallic will be picked up." She held out both hands toward him. "Won't you please stop this crazy theft! You'll get caught. Just think. It's not too late—"

The Judge cut her short. "Just leave it to me, kid. I know what I'm doing and what you don't know won't hurt you."

Polly sighed and went into the bedroom to take off her damp blouse. It had been hot at the bazaar and now she had perspired more in her anxiety over her husband. The Judge limped over to stand by the door. He seemed to want to make conversation.

"Did you buy anything? Or did they have anything to buy?"

"Too expensive," replied Polly. "Did you call room service?"

"Not yet," replied the Judge. "All I want is some Scotch and a bowl of soup."

"Don't be silly," exclaimed Polly. "We have guests. I propose to have a good meal. An Egyptian meal."

The Judge moved off into the living room and Polly picked up the phone to dial room service. As she waited for an answer she watched as the sun began to dip into the Nile. She sighed with relief that she had two hours, or just a little more, before Tina and Peter, their guests for dinner, would arrive. Somehow, someway, she had to think of some argument—even a trick—to stop the Judge from ruining himself.

She called to the Judge, "You know I am your wife and I do bear a certain responsibility for both of us."

"Don't try to meddle in my affairs." The Judge was at the door again. She turned away from him. She had not given up as she started to order dinner.

When Tina and Peter arrived, Polly had changed her dress and the Judge was pouring drinks in his shirt sleeves. Peter thought he noticed a tension in the air. Tina was fascinated to be so close to a judge, to see him informally, as he joked and laughed—maybe a little too heartily. Polly looked at her wristwatch and frowned.

"I ordered dinner for seven o'clock but it's already beyond that."

"Don't let it bother you," replied Peter. "I'm in no hurry." There was no time for her to ring the kitchen. The waiters knocked at the door. Three waiters brought with them tables, flowers for a centerpiece, silver candlesticks, appropriate china, generous gleaming flat silver, napkins, celery, olives, fresh figs, and assorted nuts. Two additional tables waited in the hall with foodstuffs. Suddenly Polly realized the waiters were moving the chair in which the mask was hidden. She saw the Judge half rise.

The Judge felt his face flush. They mustn't! He lurched forward. "That's my chair!" He smiled. "Bum leg and hip. That chair fits me. Leave it where it is."

The waiters obeyed and proceeded to finish setting the table. The head waiter turned to Polly. "Soup now? Curried duck with wedges of fresh oranges from Fayum?"

"Oh, how exotic can you get!" exclaimed Tina.

Polly smiled with pleasure and directed the waiters to proceed. The four drew up to the table and were served. Outside the last light disappeared from the surface of the Nile. The dark of evening closed over the hotel. One of the waiters lighted lamps around the room.

The Judge felt himself relax a little. Scotch now, then really good tasting soup with plenty of wine. If only Polly would keep her mouth shut. Normally she did not interfere in his affairs. She knew they were confidential. But this time she seemed to feel she knew more than he.

"I can't think of a better way to come to the end of our trip," Polly began the conversation. "New friends. Really delicious food—" she turned to the head waiter with a smile and a nod. "Luxor, Karnak, Cairo. Jewels, gold, bronze urns. No wonder this place has been the source of romance and the site of endless riches for thousands of years."

Peter leaned forward with his spoon poised. "I can't get Wilbur Mott out of my mind—speaking of riches. What in the world could he have been mixed up in to get him killed. He looked to be such a withdrawn character. He was former State Department as a matter of fact."

"You think he was trying to steal something? Or what?" asked the Judge innocently.

"Tina and I saw him at Fayum, you know. He was with an Egyptian and they had a copy or the original of what looked like a mask—"

The Judge gestured to Peter to be quiet in the presence of the waiters. Polly stood up with an "Excuse me!" Tina did not stop but continued the thoughts of the conversation. "It looked just like the mask in the Museum. Remember? That first day?"

Polly sat down again. "What is the next course?" she asked the waiter. Tina would not keep still. "Suppose Mott was planning to remove a museum piece out of the country. There's a heavy fine for that, not to mention the threat of jail. But consider the value of such an object if it did get out."

Polly began to cough. She choked on her last spoonful of soup. Tina and Peter leaned forward to help. The Judge wiped his forehead and his mouth. "Let's get on with the next course," he said. The waiter looked from Polly to the Judge and back.

Polly nodded while she struggled to get her breath again. "We don't have to hurry but if we're all finished—"

"What is the next course?" asked the Judge. "Tenderloin? Hah! That'll be the day."

"Madame asked for Egyptian food. We have roast lamb with vegetables from the Delta. There are dates and figs in wine sauce, if you wish."

"Let's try it all!" cried the Judge and tinkled his knife against his water glass. Tina almost stood up in surprise. Peter moved in his chair with his head down.

"Roger! Behave yourself! This is not a Rotary supper!"

The Judge pretended to hang his head in shame. And everyone laughed, or pretended to laugh. The waiters moved in with the lamb.

Tina commented, with fork in hand, "Peggy must be over the Atlantic by this time. I miss her. She got away before I even had the chance of a last word with her."

Polly quickly intervened. "It was such a hurry scene! I don't know how we did it!"

Peter swallowed his first piece of lamb and obviously approved. "It's too bad about that kid. Apparently she was really faithful to Dennis. It was too bad. To lose the one you've put your faith in at that age can be very disturbing. I hope her mother realizes that."

"Her aunt," injected the Judge. "Good lamb."

"Some wine sauce?" inquired Polly.

Would they never shut up, thought the Judge. He finished off his wine and waved for some more. One waiter remained to wait on them. He came forward. The Judge noted the frown on Polly's forehead and made a face at her. He was surprised at the glance Peter exchanged with Tina. Maybe he was a little drunk and probably he should stop. But it was the last night. He was almost there. And he laughed to himself. He knew something none of them knew. He knew how he intended to get the mask out of Egypt and into the United States.

"There's more salad," said Polly. How had they got to the salad? wondered the Judge to himself. He must be fading out.

"The guide book said not to eat the salad but it's so good!" muttered Tina. "I've convinced myself it's O.K." She grinned.

Peter cleared his plate of lettuce leaves and sat back. He took a deep breath of satisfaction. "Mott and Dennis. You wonder if there was some connection. And what has happened to the mask now? Did we see what we thought we saw? It is all becoming less and less meaningful. But two people have died." Peter reached over and picked up Tina's hand. "What do you think?"

"At the moment I'm content not to think. I'm content to sit and eat and drink and just be a digestive animal."

Peter shook his head. "That I'll believe when I see it."

The Judge downed another glass of wine. He addressed himself to Peter. "You don't believe it now. But every woman wants to have everything done for her. And she wants beautiful things given to her. And she wants to be made love to. That keeps them happy. All this independence and choice and full partners is just the latest ploy. It's just the latest trick to take over—" He gulped, "Take over the world. Take over—"

Tina was heard to gasp. She did stand up. "To say that I'm amazed is putting it lightly. I can't believe what I just heard. It may be time to leave." She turned to Polly. "It's been a delightful dinner—"

Polly rose and hurried to Tina. "Roger doesn't mean it. Please sit down. There's still dessert." She pressed Tina back into her chair.

Tina turned to the Judge. "I didn't imagine you were so concerned over female competition."

The Judge laughed. "Women are fools right now. In fact some of them are just plain sluts!"

Tina felt anger rise within her. Of all the people to criticize, the Judge had the least reason, given his activities of two nights ago.

The Judge tried to stand up, lost his balance, and sat down again with a grunt. "You know what a slut is? A sexually promiscuitous—promiscuis—No. It's someone who always has her wares out for sale. Doesn't matter how young. My little granddaughter, my littlest granddaughter." He paused to gain control. "Peggy is her name. Peggy, after her great aunt. She tried to seduce me—"

Polly intervened forcibly. "You don't know what you're talking about!"

"Neither do you. You're dumb! You're uninformed! You're misinformed!"

Peter and Tina exchanged glances. It became Tina's job to present excuses. "I hadn't realized it was so late! We have to call back to the States—or we'll have no one to meet us!—We have to go—"

Peter chimed in. "Dinner was such a good idea! Thanks ever so much—"

The two almost ran from the room. The waiter, who had stepped out in the hall, looked at them in astonishment as they went by. Tina tossed the comment over her shoulder to Peter, "That poor woman! Polly! If I were she I'd kill him!"

Back in the room, Polly dropped in her chair. For the moment she was alone in her whole existence. She sat alone at the table. She seemed alone in the room. The Judge whirled on her, full of words to hurt her. "You stay out of my business," he screamed. "It's my business. You'll just mess it up. You're naive and you always have been. You never really know what's going on. Now, just stay out of my way." He staggered over to the chair containing the mask and turned it upside down. The waiter opened the door a crack, decided discretion would be the better part of valor, and closed the door. Polly turned to the Judge, her trembling hands stretched out before her, along the tablecloth.

"Am I to understand from that comment that you, not Dennis, have been using Peggy? That kid. That baby!" Polly became incoherent.

"So what? What are you going to do about it?"

Polly had never been so mad in her life. The Judge wiped the back of his hand across his mouth. Polly had never been so disgusted in her life. Even his saliva was out of control. Polly suddenly was frightened of her husband. She picked up one of the knives from the table.

"And what do you think you're goin' to do with that!" sneered the Judge.

Polly threw down the knife and rushed into the bedroom. Holding onto the table for support, the Judge followed her. He caught the doorjamb to hold himself up as Polly pulled his pistol out of the top drawer in his wardrobe.

"Now, wait a minute," said the Judge. "Polly! What's gone wrong with you! Think what we can have. Peggy is the least of it. Don't be stupid—"

Polly was gasping and sobbing. The Judge distinctly heard the click as the safety catch was released.

20

The last night in Cairo.

Some of the tour group had left the hotel to eat dinner for the last night at Cairo restaurants. Others remained in the hotel packing, tired, talking with new–found friends.

The white haired lady was feeling a bit lonely. She was sitting in the lobby for the last time. The trip ended tomorrow and all the fun would be gone. There would be the long flight home, then all the mail to open and throw away. And back to the habitual grind. It's true her condo was nice and she had plenty to keep her busy. But no children, not even any grandchildren such as Bette apparently had in multiples.

She had not realized she was dozing. She jumped as the Assistant Manager bowed at the side of her chair. "May I offer you a brandy? On the Marriot. They can afford it." He laughed.

Bette and the gray haired woman arrived in the lounge together.

"Brandy? Something to drink?" The white haired lady addressed Bette and the gray haired woman. The Assistant Manager smiled and called to a passing waiter.

"Coke," said the white haired lady.

"Gin and tonic," said Bette.

"Make that two," said the gray haired woman.

The waiter bowed and went for the drinks. The Assistant Manager stood by smiling, ready to join in the conversation.

Bette started to pull out clothing from the large plastic bag she had with her. "You should have seen that bazaar. I'll bet they had a little of everything in the world!"

"It used to be the barracks for the Ottoman military guards, you know," said the white haired lady. "Can you imagine the size of the army? They scared all of Christendom."

The Assistant Manager opened his mouth to make a comment at the same time someone behind the hotel desk shouted to him in Arabic. He straightened. His eyes expressed horror. "Please, please—" He gasped, "Someone is shot. You must excuse me. Someone heard a shot upstairs." He hurried away.

Bette paid no attention. She pulled out from the shopping bag a series of matching short vests which went with short little black skirts. "I'll just show you these. Aren't they cute? I have to pack up all this stuff and Joe is ready to have kittens. Just look at these."

The gray haired woman felt the raised needlework on the vest and nodded her head in approval. The white haired lady rose and turned to look after the figure of the Assistant Manager. He had disappeared. She sat on the arm of the chair.

Joe appeared on the marble stairs leading from the casino. He was pulling along with him a large box. "Oh, so there you are." He panted to a stop in front of Bette. "This is the smallest they have. I'll have to cut it down or we won't be able to carry it." Bette got up with a sigh just as the waiter appeared with the drinks.

"Something to drink?" said the white haired lady to Joe.

"No, no. I have to go to work now. You ladies have had your fun. My turn has come."

The waiter passed the drinks and hurried across the room to the desk. Excited Arabic could be heard.

"He really likes to do this," said Bette as she followed Joe down the stairs, glass in hand.

"It's too bad. It's almost all over," said the gray haired woman.

"In some respects I'm glad it's about over. We've had two deaths. That's a lot for a small tour like this." The white haired lady sampled her drink. "With us gone things may calm down."

"Oh, I suppose so," replied the gray haired woman. "Just the same, it's been fun—as well as gruesome. I'd never have a chance at a dead body at home."

"I should hope not!" exclaimed the white haired lady with a grin.

"I don't know why I'm not scared," mused the gray haired woman. "Must be the Egyptian air or something."

At that moment Polly suddenly appeared on the stairs which descended to the lounge at the other side of the room. Her clothing was rumpled and she was sobbing and crying. "Where is Peter—or Tina? Have you seen them? I've got to find one or the other of them—or both. Oh, God! God!"

The white haired lady stood up. The gray haired woman started toward her to help. "What is wrong? Something is terribly wrong."

Polly pulled herself up and started down the stairs again. "The Judge is dead."

"What?" said the gray haired woman.

"I shot him," cried Polly and disappeared down the stairs. They heard her begin to laugh hysterically.

CHAPTER

21

Do justice for the Lord of Justice . . .
Keep away from wrong doing . . .
For justice is for eternity.

Inspector Hakim looked around his office with disgust. His wife kept their apartment far cleaner and his son was far more orderly than his assistant with whom he shared the office. The walls had never been painted in ten years and all the furniture squeaked. But what he objected to the most was the practice of throwing files and papers and reports on his desk, helter skelter, when he was not present, which meant he had to dig to the bottom of the pile—usually—to reach what he wanted. He sighed, sat down, and dug to the bottom of the pile.

The file in his hand was titled Roger Poland/Pauline Poland, USA—Homicide. He checked the small sheet attached to the front with a paper clip. It was signed and sealed by the proper authority and authorized the arrest of Pauline Poland and her delivery into custody forthwith. He

161

opened the file and found facing him a photocopy of the ticket of Pauline Poland to fly from Egypt to Paris at 8:07 A.M. tomorrow morning. Via KLM. It was 4:00 P.M. so he had less than twenty-four hours to complete his investigation.

There was no doubt. He wished he had not given up smoking. That was what he needed to do while he reviewed the evidence and statements he had accumulated.

He knew to start that Peter and Tina Carson, in whose intelligence and veracity he had complete confidence, were totally convinced that Polly had killed her husband in self defense. (In his mind she would always be Polly. A nice woman, a nice mother. Why did he have to admire her!)

The worst of it was that he did admire her. She had rid the world of a disgrace. The more he investigated the worse it got. Some part of the respect for "THE LAW" which was the mainstay of British organization had stuck with Inspector Hakim. He grimaced both at the thought of Judge Poland and the thought of a man shot by his own wife. This man, a judge, had poisoned a sexual rival and was perhaps guilty of other crimes and misdemeanors in connection with his judicial responsibilities. But a wife owed a special degree of care and love to the man she had married and by whom she had had children. Or were either of those two thoughts appropriate to a murderess? What a horrible name to call Polly!

The Inspector reached to the corner of his desk and picked up the small, miniature statue of the god Horus which customarily sat there. The representation of the god was genuine, dating officially to the Eighteenth Dynasty. An archaeologist from the Pickett Expedition three years ago had given it to him in thanks for his help. He turned the little falcon in his hand and rubbed the beak. Hakim was neither Muslim nor Christian but he did not believe in the old gods either. Yet there was something about Horus one could not disregard easily. Egypt was shaped under the aegis of the little fellow, one eye representing the sun and the other the moon. He mused on the thought that Horus on occasion had taken the lives presented to him into his own hands without regard for the law.

His mind turned to Peggy. On the one hand Peggy had been totally candid in his telephone interview with her. The Inspector had to admit (to himself) that he was a little shocked to hear that she and Dennis regularly slept together. The only reason the Judge was not involved was that Dennis made sure he was always in bed first. He checked again the fact sheet in the file on Peggy. Yes, it did. It did say "15 years of age." God! he thought. His ancestors had followed such practices, but supposedly this American girl knew differently. To say nothing of AIDS.

And then there was the question of Mott. How did he fit in? Three people were dead: Mott, by reason of a beating which killed him (according to the medicals); Dennis by poison, strychnine to be specific, administered in a Coke can; Judge Poland by shooting. Certainly there was no common method or place. For Judge Poland it may have been self defense— except, except for one point. He had been shot in the back.

He would have said the deaths were all unconnected, that he would be justified in continuing his investigation into the death of Mott at his leisure, that the Judge killed Dennis and that Polly had shot the Judge in self-defense. Again except— except for the mask! He opened his top drawer and peaked into the rear area. There it was. Dull in the dimness of the drawer but glinting, in weighty richness. Polly had given it to him for safekeeping. He thought: Was there a common thread which ran from the mask through Mott, Dennis and the Judge? "Query" as the barristers said.

At that point, Suzie opened the door without knocking to announce Mr. Carson was outside. Suzie was his secretary but

Suzie was not her name. She watched too many American movies and serial soaps, with the result she dressed like her idols, tried to talk like them and was equally, in Hakim's mind, graceless and offensive. Some day he would discharge her for opening his door without knocking—but not today. Peter Carson appeared beside Suzie, but he had enough courtesy to ask, "O.K. to bother you?"

Hakim rose with his smile and welcomed Peter to a chair.

"I won't take a minute." Peter did not sit down. "We have forgotten to tell you something. I'm sorry but it slipped our minds. Tina just remembered as she was packing our stuff to go home." Peter placed in Hakim's outstretched hand the two notes of pasted newsprint "NOT YOUR BUSINESS" and "WE MEAN YOU." "I have no idea what they mean or even if they have anything to do with this but we thought you should have them. That one was under our door when we returned from that trip to Fayum. We found the other after dinner the first night."

Inspector Hakim studied the notes, both sides, looked at Peter and looked at the notes again. Finally he asked, "Who occupied the rooms on either side of you?"

"I thought of that," replied Peter, "And I meant to find out but I never did. I questioned the room clerk but he was not helpful. So I have no idea who had rooms around us. Not even who was on the same floor."

"Do you remember your room number?"

Peter could respond to that question. "917. Right on the corner where the security guard sometimes sat."

Hakim's spine stiffened. "What security guard?"

"Most of the time when we came in there was a man who sat in a kind of alcove next to the door of our room. We assumed he was a security guard. We figured they didn't trust Americans. With good reason it appears."

"There was no security guard," commented Hakim.

"Honestly?" questioned Peter and sat down in the chair to which he had been waved when he had entered Hakim's office. "The plot thickens."

"Maybe you have something here. I don't know what for sure. But we constantly are having to deal with thieves who want to steal and remove our antiquities. It has become quite disgusting. As you are well aware they can be valuable and in this case that mask is worth a king's ransom. A pharaoh's ransom, I should say. That it should cause three deaths would not be out of line."

"Dennis was in the import-export business in San Francisco," said Peter. "The possibility of connection is obvious. I never thought of it until this minute."

"San Francisco? Oriental?"

"Not necessarily, as I understand it. Both New York and San Francisco are great import cities."

"This pasting on the notes is a universal method to avoid handwriting experts," commented Hakim. "But the newsprint is in English and the paper itself is American recycled. Americans are the only ones so far who commonly use recycled paper in international production. So we know we have an American or someone with access to American newsprint."

Peter interrupted. "You know we told you we saw Mott at Fayum with the mask—we thought. It was after that that the note was slipped under our door, I think. To me that means Mott called someone at the hotel to scare us off."

"I ask was the 'security guard' in place when you found the note?"

"Nooo. He wasn't. I remember I looked out in the hall but no one was to be seen."

Hakim mumbled under his breath. "Security guard. Where does he fit in? Why by your door?"

"Wait a minute!" exclaimed, Peter. "When we arrived the Judge was furious and held us all up at registration because he had ordered a suite and they did not give him a suite. He wanted a room for Peggy, one for himself and his wife, and a sitting room between. Tina practically fell asleep on top of me while we waited."

"So his room was changed and you were moved into what was to have been his room."

"Could be." Peter's face expressed puzzlement.

"Let me propose a hypothesis," commenced Hakim. "Mott picked up the mask at Fayum." At that point Hakim opened his desk drawer that held the mask. He continued slowly. "He thought you were after the mask as well. He phoned ahead to an accomplice to scare you off (as you said), the notes were left under your door—And could it be that the accomplice in the end did away with Wilbur Mott?" Hakim brought the mask from his desk drawer and placed it on the desk blotter next to the little bust of Horus.

Peter stood up; he almost gasped. He spoke in a whisper. "I can see what the problem is." It seemed as if a gold sparkling light filled the room. It was alive, warm, arresting. Both the men were fascinated. Peter seemed frozen, his eyes riveted to the mask. Like the Judge before him he was overwhelmed by the beauty and the grace of the mask.

"Oddly enough," mused Hakim, "the two objects represent the same time period." He rearranged the relative positions of Horus and the mask to put them closer together. "Interestingly enough, Horus represents life after death and the mask is the depiction of death itself."

Peter scratched the end of his nose where some skin was peeling off from too much exposure to the sun. "Don't we have to agree that we don't know who killed Mott and that we do know that the Judge killed Dennis? What is important is whether Polly is to be held for trial for killing the Judge—or released because she was defending herself. As I understand it, Egypt recognizes self defense."

Hakim answered slowly, haltingly. "We have Polly's word for the self defense and the fact the Judge was shot in the back for the medical fact. Do they conflict or not?"

"Not necessarily." Peter looked very certain of himself. "The Judge could have turned during a struggle. He turned at the moment Polly pulled the trigger."

"A third party. Consider a third party. It holds together better." For the first time Hakim sounded excited. "The same person who killed Mott also shot the Judge."

"But Polly—" began Peter.

Hakim interrupted. "Polly admits she was struggling with the Judge. She might not have noticed. The revolver she had was fired but there could have been another gun and another person. I'm not sure we checked the ballistics of the spent bullet we found in the wall, against the bullet in Polly's gun."

Peter frowned and made a face. "Too easy. We don't know if there was—is—a third person and we for sure don't know who he is. Sheer conjecture."

Hakim disagreed. "Your 'security guard' was arrested for loitering at the hotel the day you left. That's how I knew about him. His history is interesting. He was part of the security for Nasser, our former president." He raised his eyebrows. "After which he became involved in the illegal acquisition—shall we say—of antiquities. Interested?"

Peter tossed his head. "You're holding out on me, as we say. I suppose you have him in custody and his confession is in that file."

Hakim laughed. "We are not so lucky. He has disappeared. That to me is very informative. It will be difficult to find him as long as he stays hidden. But eventually he will emerge and then we will catch and interrogate him. I will not be surprised—yes. Yes I think he is a likely prospect."

Peter studied Hakim for a moment, his eyes narrowed. "I think I get it. You would prefer not to be involved with a tourist if you can avoid it. Particularly a judge's wife."

Hakim smiled. He would never let anyone know that he wanted to avoid hurting Polly, if he could, and still be true to his responsibility as police for Egypt. "There are a number of considerations," he said.

All further discussions had to come to an end because Suzie once again opened the door without knocking and ushered in Tina and Polly. Both the men stood. "Thank you, Suzie," said Hakim. Tina caught Peter's hand and held it close to her side.

Peter started the conversation without any delay. "Inspector Hakim has developed some interesting evidence. There is another person in this. The police know who he is but he is in hiding for now." He spoke directly to Polly. "You may not have fired the shot responsible for the Judge's death."

"If I could believe that—Oh, if I could believe that!" exclaimed Polly. "The one thing I cannot begin to imagine is how I will explain to the family what happened." She lifted her hand to her mouth as if to bite the forefinger of her right hand. "It's not like me! I'm not a violent person. I don't even usually lose my temper."

Hakim interrupted. "If I am correct the shot was actually fired from the balcony or from someone just behind you. Someone completely unknown to you. The same person who killed Mr. Mott. You, therefore, are completely innocent." Tina tightened her hand around Peter's hand and he responded in like fashion.

Polly was speechless; finally she managed to say: "I came to give myself up. Tina said that was the best thing I could do.

Then she and Peter would go to the American Consulate on my behalf."

Hakim took the arrest paper off the top of his file, tore it into pieces and put it and the paper clip into his pants pocket. "You are free to go. All of you. I am just sorry as an Egyptian that your visit was so—so traumatic."

For several moments no one knew what to say or do. Peter put out his hand and he and Hakim shook hands, then hugged each other briefly. "If you ever come to the States and to the Midwest, look us up. I mean it. Please do!"

Tina pushed aside Hakim's offer of his hand, put her arms around him and kissed him on the cheek. "You will always be my favorite Egyptian."

Hakim looked at Polly and Polly dropped her glance. She put out her hand and looked up. Her eyes caught his eyes and held. Hakim took her hand, then pulled her close to him, and kissed her. "May your God be with you for the rest of your life!" He stepped back and as they left the office he very slowly slipped the mask into the desk drawer and carefully replaced the little statue of Horus on the corner of his desk. As always the little falcon represented life and not death to Hakim. He sighed. He was in charge of life and death so often.

He sat down and dug the next file out from under the papers on his desk.

ACKNOWLEDGMENTS

The trip sequence and some chapter epigraphs were suggested by Abercrombie & Kent, *Travel Itinerary: The Nile Explorer*, 1992.

The dedicatory quotation concerning the law is due to Sir Edward Coke in his *Institutes*, 1628.

The poetic speech in chapter 9 and the epigraphs for chapters 9 and 21 are taken from the Eighth Petition of "The Eloquent Peasant" (Middle Kingdom), excerpted on p. 181 of Miriam Lichtheim's *Ancient Egyptian Literature*, Vol. 1: *The Old and Middle Kingdoms*, University of California Press, 1975. The same volume on p. 168 contains the excerpt from "The Dispute between a Man and His Ba" used as the epigraph for chapter 13.

Manfred Lurker's *The Gods and Symbols of Ancient Egypt: An Illustrated Dictionary*, Thames and Hudson, Inc., 1982 provided numerous useful references and reminders of the multiplicity of interpretation given to artifacts of ancient Egypt.

Kay Showker's *Fodor's 91 Egypt: A Practical and Historical Guide*, Fodor's Travel Publications, Inc., 1991, was helpful in setting the stage for the events and places a tourist of the late twentieth century may have encountered. Our epigraph for chapter 2 is taken from page 113.

J. E. Manchip White's *Ancient Egypt, Its Culture and History*, Dover Publications, Inc. 1970, interpreted general historical background. Several summaries such as Hada's discussion of the evolution of the pyramids in chapter 7 are patterned on his account.

Uta C. Merzbach rendered valuable assistance during the final stages of manuscript preparation.

Special thanks are due to Miriam Freer, Gretchen Needham, and Christyann Rothmel at Puritan Press for their talented collaboration and unusual help with the book's production; to Jan Siers for providing a cheerful presence and efficient support; and to Fred Lyford, whose immediate response presented a humane voice and an appreciation for the tradition of the printed word.

Shirley Surrette Duffy, a native of Gloucester, Massachusetts, earned her undergraduate and graduate degrees at Emerson College before engaging in postgraduate studies at the Louisiana State University. Her two major affiliations during a long teaching career were with the Radford School in El Paso, Texas, where she taught dramatic arts and served as Dean of Girls, and with the North Shore Community College in Massachusetts, from which she retired as Professor of English in 1992. Her primary research interest lies in literature that mirrors an author's regional surroundings. Her publications include articles on the comparative literature of Essex County, England, and Essex County, Massachusetts. She has been active in civic affairs, counts travel among her numerous interests, but retains her lifelong love for Cape Ann, home to five generations of her ancestors.

Florence E. Freeman was a graduate of the Wilmington Friends School in Wilmington, Delaware, Wellesley College, and the University of Pennsylvania Law School. She practiced corporate law in Delaware for several years before opening her own law practice in Weston, Massachusetts, where she served as town counsel for eighteen years.

She was the first president of the Weston Drama Workshop where she directed several plays. Her other nonprofessional interests included history, archeology, and detective fiction. She was an experienced sailor and loved to travel. After her retirement in Weston, she took up year-round residence in Gloucester, where she had summered since childhood and where she died in 2004.

The authors' shared love of travel led to the idea of a joint work on Egypt.